OUTAGE

POWERLESS NATION BOOK ONE

OUTAGE

POWERLESS NATION ϟ BOOK ONE

ELLISA BARR

This is a work of fiction. Names, characters, organizations, places, events, and incidents are either products of the author's imagination or are used fictitiously.

Published by Skyscape, New York

www.apub.com

Amazon, the Amazon logo, and Skyscape are trademarks of Amazon.com, Inc., or its affiliates.

ISBN-13: 9781477829943
ISBN-10: 1477829946

Cover design by Cyanotype Book Architects

Library of Congress Control Number: 2014959253

Printed in the United States of America

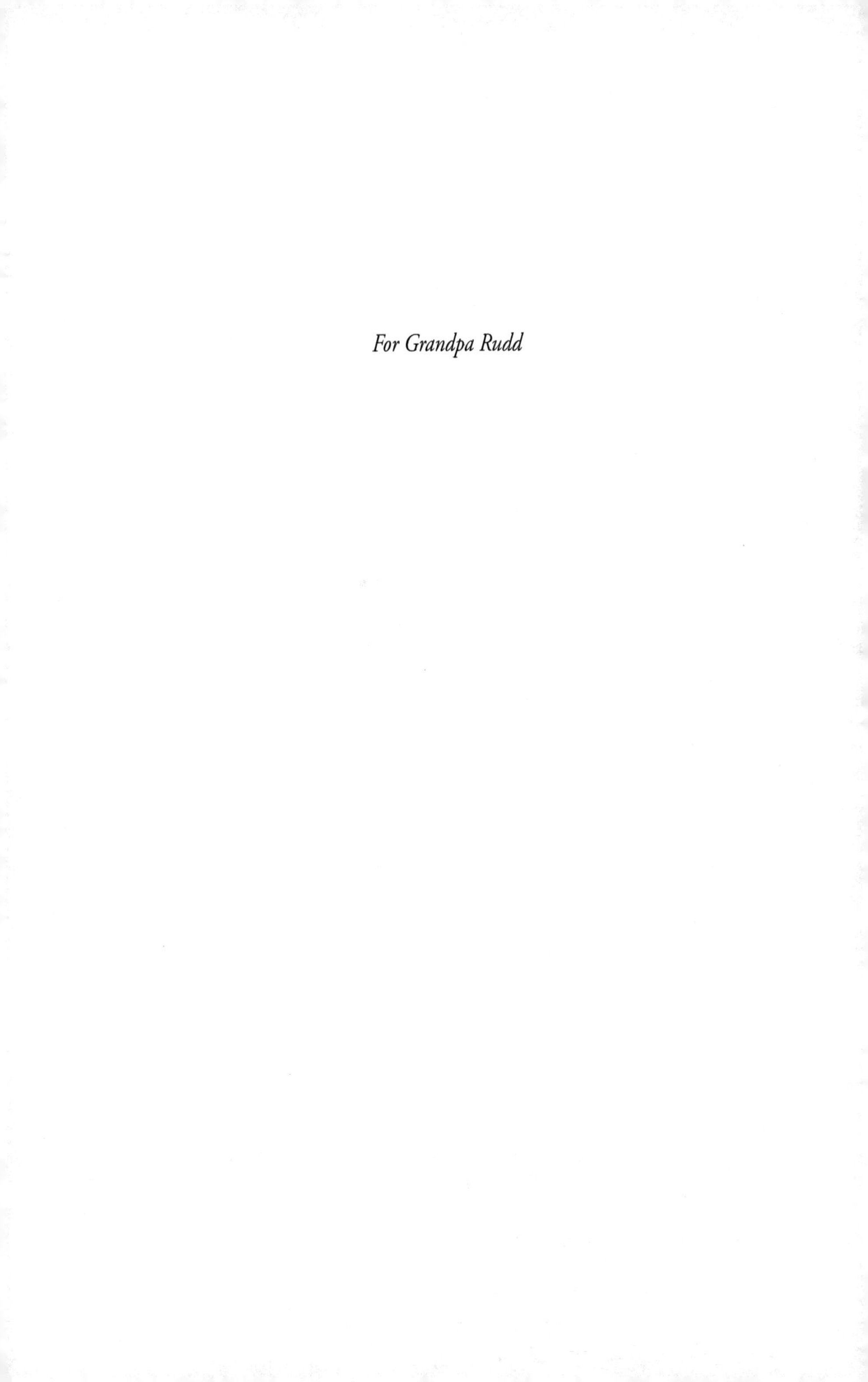

For Grandpa Rudd

For God hath not given us the spirit of fear; but of power, and of love, and of a sound mind.

2 Timothy 1:7

CHAPTER ONE

Dee sat outside the farmhouse and peeled slivers of paint from the old porch swing. Inside, she could hear her parents talking to her grandpa and getting ready to leave. They were going on a cruise and leaving her on a tiny, run-down farm in the backwoods of northern Washington.

She sat still and listened when her mom's voice dropped to a whisper. "Thanks so much for doing this. I just . . . just need to get away. You have no idea."

Grandpa chuckled. "You might be surprised. Don't forget I raised four kids of my own."

"Oh, Dad, things are different now. She's on her phone constantly. Even when she's home it's like she's not there. She hasn't talked to me about anything important since . . . Well, since, you know."

Her grandpa's voice was reassuring. "She'll come around; you just need to give her time."

"Well, a week is a good start. Maybe she'll make up her mind to have some fun."

"I hope so, and I hope you do, too. Which ports are you stopping in?"

Dee lost interest in the conversation and stared at the farm without seeing it. She wished they would hurry up and go so she didn't have to listen to anything else about Alaska. You'd think it was the Bahamas or something, not just a bunch of ice and rocks.

She felt the porch swing rock as her dad sat down next to her, but she kept peeling paint and resisting the urge to check her phone for new messages. There wasn't any reception out here, and as soon as her parents left she was taking the old man's truck into town to look for a hotspot, and maybe even a bus station that would sell her a ticket back home.

"I'm going to miss you," her dad said.

Dee gave him a flat look she hoped would convey utter disbelief, but he kept talking.

"I know it's been a tough year, Dee, and I'm sorry I haven't been around more. It's been hard for all of us, but I should have been there for you."

Dee kept her gaze straight ahead, but she could feel a traitorous tear forming at the corner of one eye.

"When we get back from this trip, things are going to be different," he said. "I'm going to tell my boss I can't travel so much. I know it'll take a while, but we're going to be a family again. Would you like that?"

Dee gave a half shrug. There was no way they'd be a family again.

He put an arm around her and gave her a squeeze. "Don't give up on us, kiddo. We will never, ever give up on you."

He stood up, and Dee wanted to yell that he *had* given up on her. Dumping her at Grandpa's house in the middle of nowhere while they went off on a vacation was the definition of giving up. She wanted to say it, but she was afraid her one tear would turn into an uncontrollable flood.

Her mom came out and stood in front of the swing for a long moment. Then she put a hand under Dee's chin and lifted it until daughter was looking into mother's eyes. Dee's gaze slid away to look at a spot above her mom's left ear.

"Maddie," she said. "Just look at me for a minute." Her voice faltered. "Please?"

Dee met her mom's gaze with hostility. She wished they would just go.

Her mom took a deep breath and Dee braced for a lecture, but her mom surprised her. "I love you, Maddie. No matter what you do, no matter what happens. I will always love you." Then she gave her a kiss on the cheek. Dee was so surprised she didn't even remember to flinch away.

Her parents were waving at her from the car now, and somehow she was waving back. Part of her wanted to run after them and beg them not to leave, but the other part just wanted them gone so they would stop pretending things could ever be the same.

*

She was surprised when her grandfather put on his boots and said he was going out. "I've got to go check on a sick cow down to Louisville, so you just make yourself at home and I'll be back in time for dinner."

This confused Dee briefly. It wasn't even nine in the morning. Was he leaving her alone all day? He must have seen her confusion because he reminded her, "Dinner on the farm is around two. Maybe you could whip us up something to eat? There's some bacon and eggs in the fridge and plenty of food in the pantry."

Did he really think she was going to be his personal chef? Nuking some nachos was pretty much her limit when it came to cooking, and she hadn't seen a microwave in his kitchen, just an old gas stove. That thing was probably dangerous—no way was she going near it.

"Don't worry, old Jasper will be here to keep an eye on things." He meant the black-and-white Shetland sheepdog that was eyeing the pickup hopefully. Then to Jasper he said, "Guard the farm, boy." Jasper stopped wagging his tail and sat dutifully at the foot of the front steps. A few minutes later, Dee had the farm to herself.

"I guess I'll go take a look around," she told the dog, "since my ride into town just drove away." He responded with a wag of his tail and followed her inside.

Dee had actually wanted to poke around her grandfather's place, truth be told. She didn't know much about architecture but she figured it was a fairly traditional farmhouse. Most of the downstairs was taken up by a combined living room and dining room. There was a woodstove at one end of the long room and a doorway leading to her grandfather's office.

She tried the doorknob of the office and went inside. Dee bit her lip when she saw how he'd decorated the space. School art projects and homemade cards that she and Jacob had made filled the walls. She saw a handprint turkey she'd made in second grade and placed her fifteen-year-old hand over her seven-year-old hand. Jacob had made one that year, too, and his traced hand was even smaller.

Dee made herself stop staring at the tiny handprint and scanned the rest of the room. A large desk and leather chair took up most of the space, along with file cabinets and a bookshelf filled with Louis L'Amour Westerns and books on farming. She looked through the desk drawers and wondered where her grandpa kept his computer. He had to have a computer, right? She couldn't find one, though, and when she checked her phone she didn't see any wireless networks, either.

No texting and now no email? "This isn't happening," she muttered to herself as she left the office.

She missed her friends desperately. They'd been mortified when she told them her parents were shipping her off to middle-of-nowhere Washington for a week. "What do they even do there? Cow tipping?"

"Maybe you'll meet someone," said Natalie. She was Dee's best friend.

"As if," said Dee. "Like I'm going to fall for some country music–lovin' bumpkin."

"I didn't say you had to fall for him. Just a hookup, you know?" She reached into her purse. "See this stick of gum? It's lucky. When you find the guy you want to kiss, just pop it in your mouth and the lucky gum will do the rest."

Dee had laughed and put the gum in her pocket. She patted the pocket now and wished Natalie was here.

She wandered into the kitchen. It was already her favorite room in the house, and Jasper clearly agreed with her. He ran to his own little bed tucked away under a tall side table while she looked around. The kitchen was painted a pale yellow with sage-green crown molding and window trim. White, airy curtains were pulled aside, letting sunlight fill the east-facing room and brighten the older appliances and worn butcher-block countertops.

Yellow daisies were tucked into an old-fashioned Coke bottle. She touched one—yes, it was real. Was her grandfather sentimental about flowers? A huge table took up most of the other half of the room and there was a large antique-style map on the wall next to it. Dee had a sudden vision of her mother doing homework at the table while her grandmother made dinner on the old gas stove.

A door leading off the kitchen led down a short hallway to her grandfather's room. She went inside and stood in front of the vanity. Tiny perfume bottles were organized on the surface, and Dee breathed in their old-fashioned fragrances.

She sat at the table and looked at herself in the mirror. Straight brown hair reached below her shoulders and hazel eyes gazed back defensively at her. *Not much to see there.* She stood and went out.

Dee picked up an apple from the bowl in the kitchen and polished it on her shirt while she wondered what to do next. It was only nine thirty in the morning and she was already bored. What was she supposed to do all day with no phone and no Internet? In the end she settled for one of her grandpa's Westerns about a couple of young kids who lived through an Indian attack and had to survive in the wilderness while they tried to find help.

"I wouldn't make it one day in the wilderness," she told Jasper. "In fact, I'm not sure I can make it one day without a dishwasher. Better hope I can find some paper plates."

It was getting close to "dinnertime" (she mentally added air quotes to the word), and although she had no intention of cooking a meal, she decided to see what the food situation was. First she checked the fridge and saw a couple of eggs. They looked normal enough, even though she knew they came from Grandpa's own chickens. Somehow she'd expected farm-fresh eggs to be covered with some kind of gross chicken slime. The milk was in a glass bottle, and she could see a thin layer of something resting on top of the liquid. Dee wrinkled her nose. Cereal was out, too.

She spotted the bacon he'd mentioned and then looked at the knobs on the gas stove for a few minutes. This morning Grandpa had used a match to light it, and with her luck she'd probably blow the whole thing up. No, thanks.

Sorry, bacon. It's not you; it's me.

Jasper, who hadn't taken his eyes off the bacon since she'd gotten it out of the fridge, saw her put it away and gave a sad dog groan as he put his head back down on his paws.

Maybe there would be something she could make that didn't require cooking. When she opened the door of the pantry she saw just the thing: home-canned pears. She picked up the jar and glanced at the rest of the shelves, taking in cans of soup and a few tins of tuna and chicken as well as more jars of home canning. There wasn't a lot, but she supposed it was more than enough for one old bachelor. She wondered if anyone would deliver a pizza this far out.

When Grandpa got home he didn't seem bothered by the fact that she didn't have dinner waiting for him. He just asked how her day had been and started assembling frying pans and breakfast ingredients.

"I know it's not fancy, but since your grandma died without letting me in on any of her cooking secrets, I'm afraid it's been back to basics around here." He glanced over at Dee. "Did you inherit the chef gene, by chance?"

Dee shook her head. "Not even a little. The year I turned eleven my mom actually requested as her Mother's Day gift that I *not* make her breakfast in bed." Jacob had been nine that year. Dee had been sure she could pull off a tasty surprise breakfast despite her mom's request, but Jacob suggested they paint a picture of a breakfast and bring that up on a tray instead. She could still hear her mom's laughter.

Grandpa's back was to her while he fried bacon, but she heard him say, "Why don't you go on out and get us some fresh eggs."

Just great, thought Dee. The only other time she'd gone near the chickens, they crowded around and pecked at her painted toenails. She was about to decline but remembered seeing Grandpa pull the truck in near the coop. He'd be busy for a few minutes. This might be her chance.

"Just going to get my sweater!" she called as she ran upstairs to get her backpack and money.

Her room upstairs had a dormer window with a view of the mountains and a soft, cozy rug over the wood flooring. The pipe for the woodstove was against one wall, and the bedspread on the antique four-poster was a thick quilt her grandmother had made. Dee thought the room was pretty nice, even for an old house, and she might have let herself enjoy it just a little except her plan was to get back to civilization as soon as she could get her hands on the keys to her grandpa's truck.

She stuffed a change of clothes into the backpack and then opened the drawer where she'd hidden her money. Even though she was in a hurry, Dee couldn't resist unzipping the wallet and looking at the bills folded neatly inside. It was her entire life savings accumulated from babysitting jobs, allowances, birthday money, and unclaimed dollar bills from around her house. She didn't have to count it to know she had a little over three hundred dollars. After she bought the bus ticket she'd still have at least fifty dollars, which would be enough to take a taxi from the bus terminal in Maryland to her house. It was worth every penny to get out of this one-horse town.

Dee slung the pack over one shoulder and headed downstairs, where the smell of bacon made her stomach growl. She couldn't see into the kitchen from the bottom of the steps so she called out, "Going to get those eggs now." Her mom would have been suspicious, but Grandpa just called back a wordless affirmative.

She hadn't seen him come in with keys and figured that he probably kept them in the truck. She almost held her breath as she crossed the front yard to the coop and the truck parked next to it. It was an older model Chevrolet with a springy bench seat covered by a rough blanket. Her heart flipped when she saw she was right about the keys. There they were, sitting in the ignition. One turn and she'd be on her way out of here. Dee felt a vague sense of disquiet at abandoning her grandpa, but he was used to being on his own, right? And she wasn't staying here one minute longer than she had to. She turned the key, expecting to hear the engine turn over.

Click. Nothing happened.

She tried again. Nothing.

"Piece of crap truck!" She hit the steering wheel in fury. That's when she noticed the gear shifter.

"Duh," she berated herself. It was a manual transmission. She had never driven one, but she understood the basic principle and wondered if it would be anything like a dirt bike. Natalie's older brother had once tried to teach her to drive one, but spent most of the time laughing at her for stalling it.

She clutched and braked at the same time and gave the engine another try. It spluttered, then died. Twice more it did that, then she gave it some gas and it caught on the next try. She thought for a minute, and then put the vehicle in first gear. "Clutch off, gas on." The truck lurched forward and then stalled again. This wasn't going so well.

A figure appeared suddenly at her window and she jumped in surprise. Grandpa scratched his head in apparent consternation. "You know when I said to go get eggs, I didn't mean from the store."

Dee was about to make up a lie when she saw a quirk of his lips that she thought might hide a smile. She stammered, lost for an answer, but nothing came out.

"If you'll let me give you a driving lesson or two, you can take the truck into town tomorrow. I know spending time with an old codger isn't your idea of fun. Maybe you can meet some of the young folks hereabouts."

"Oh Grandpa, you're not a codger." Considering him for a moment, she thought to herself that he wasn't bad for an old guy. He wasn't treating her like her parents and other adults did, as if she might break at any moment.

He continued, "School's out for the summer, and I'm sure there will be some kids your age at the movie theater tomorrow afternoon. Why don't you give them a chance?"

She wasn't remotely interested in making friends with a bunch of country losers, but she'd humor him for now. "Let me think about it, okay?" she said.

"Fair enough," he replied.

Now that she had permission to take the truck, she just needed to learn how to drive it. "Can I still take you up on that driving lesson?"

"I thought you'd never ask. Scoot over."

CHAPTER TWO

The next day, after he did the farm chores, Grandpa came inside and made a pot of coffee and poured them each a cup. Dee sat at the table and wondered how her parents were. They'd be at sea all day today. She watched Grandpa skim some of the thick layer off the top of the milk and stir it into his coffee. She realized it must be fresh cream and wondered how it tasted—not enough to try it, though. The sunlit kitchen was peaceful and surprisingly homey. Dee couldn't remember the last time she'd enjoyed a quiet moment with her mom.

After a while Grandpa said, "Sitting here like this reminds me an awful lot of your grandma. You look like her, you know. I can show you some pictures of her in high school when you get back. If you'd like."

Dee realized showing her the photos was a big deal to him and she felt a real pang of conscience about leaving. Maybe it wouldn't be so bad to stay for a few days. She'd think about it. But she was still going to check out the bus terminal and make sure she was right about the price of a ticket to Maryland.

She nodded and changed the subject. "So do you think I can get the truck down to the road without stalling it?"

"Not a chance," he responded, and Dee laughed because she had no doubt he was right.

*

The lane was rutted and the old truck bounced along until she finally came to the main road, if you could call it that. With the windows down and music blaring from the radio (even if it was country music), Dee had the road to herself and felt free in a way she hadn't felt for months.

Up ahead she saw someone in the distance. As she got closer the figure put out his thumb for a ride and Dee hesitated. It was a guy, and he didn't seem old or threatening. He was carrying an enormous backpack that looked heavy. She probably shouldn't give him a ride, though; her mom would hate it.

With that thought, Dee slowed and pulled to a stop alongside the hitchhiker.

The young man rested his tanned forearms on the passenger side door and leaned partway in through the window. He wasn't as old as she'd thought. Maybe a year or two older than she was, so about seventeen. Long eyelashes framed dark eyes, and the stubbly shadow of a beard darkened his chin. His gaze was amused as he asked, "Didn't your parents teach you not to pick up strange guys on deserted highways?"

Dee's retort came easily to her lips. "Why do you think I stopped?"

"Oh, a rebel—a girl after my own heart."

She hated being judged so quickly and accurately and it made her sharp. "Do you want a ride or not?"

In answer, the young man said, "I'm Mason," and slung his backpack into the bed of the truck and got in beside her.

Dee started a silent chant in her head (*don't-stall-don't-stall-don't-stall*) and coolly tried to ease the truck into first gear.

"Dang it," she cursed under her breath a moment later.

It took two more failed tries and a big lurch before the truck was on its way, and Dee could feel her cheeks blazing with heat. Why had she picked this guy up, anyway?

"First time driving a stick?" He didn't *sound* like he was laughing at her.

"No." The engine made a terrible grinding sound as she tried to find third gear. It was hopeless. The diagram on the stick shift distinctly showed that you had to slide it to the right and forward to get into gear, but it refused to go.

"Easy, now." Mason covered her hand with his large tan one. His hand was warm on hers and when she glanced at him in surprise, she saw his eyes were friendly, not mocking. "The problem is you keep trying to put it in reverse. Instead, just go straight up toward the radio. See?"

The truck slid smoothly into third gear and he released her hand. Dee sighed with relief.

"Not your first time, eh?" A teasing tone had crept into his voice.

"If you don't like my driving, I'd be happy to let you out here."

"I think your driving is fantastic. It's just your shifting that could use a little work." The truck let out a grinding sound of agreement as she tried for fourth. The timing of it was too perfect and Dee couldn't hold back a giggle.

"Okay, maybe it's my second time."

Mason's smile lit up his face. "Don't worry, you'll get it with some practice. This is a great old truck. Is it yours?"

"No, it belongs to my grandfather. He's a farmer."

"That would explain the tools in back."

Dee appreciated that he was trying to make conversation, but it was all kind of awkward, especially since she had to concentrate on changing gears.

"I take it you're just visiting, then?" said Mason.

"You're full of questions, aren't you?"

Maybe it had been a bad idea to stop for him. In Maryland she wouldn't have dreamed of picking up a hitchhiker, but knowing she was heading back home soon had made her reckless. Dee glanced at her passenger again. He was wearing jeans and a black T-shirt that fit him snugly. Natalie would approve of his well-muscled physique even though he looked dusty and tired. She wondered how long he'd been walking.

She changed the subject. "Do you know where the bus station is in Lookout Falls?"

"Bus station?" he asked, drawing out the words.

"Yeah, you know," she said, "as in the station where the buses are?"

"I know what a bus station is," he said, not seeming the least put out by her tone. "Just trying to think if there's one closer than Spokane."

"Spokane?" said Dee, not quite keeping a wail out of her voice. "What about Louisville?" That was the next town past Lookout Falls.

"It's not 'Loo-ee-ville.' Around here we say 'Loo-iss-ville.' They've got the nearest McDonald's, but no bus terminal. Anyway, why would you need a bus when you've got this amazing truck?"

"Somehow I doubt it could get me all the way to Maryland," Dee said wryly. "I'd end up like you, with my thumb out, hoping a serial killer didn't pick me up."

"Uh-oh, should I be scared?" said Mason, sliding away from her and against the door.

"Of course. Don't you know I'm taking you back to my lair to dismember you?"

"Your lair at the bus station in Spokane?"

"If only," she said. "It looks like I'm only going as far as Lookout Falls today. Sorry I can't take you farther."

"No problem," said Mason. "I don't have to be anywhere."

"Where are you headed, anyway?"

"Around."

"Are you far from home?" she tried again.

"Not far enough."

Dee glanced over at him. His lips were pressed together in a thin line and his hands were clenched in fists so tight his knuckles were white. She'd obviously touched on a sensitive subject and she searched for something to say to lighten the mood.

"So is there anything fun to do around here?"

"Well, there's hitchhi—"

"*Besides* hitchhiking," said Dee.

"Not really, then, no. Unless you like to skateboard. There's a pretty nice skate park in Lookout Falls."

"Do I strike you as a skater girl?"

"You've got the angry rebel thing down all right, but if you're not into skating there's always farming. There's a *lot* of farming around here." He emphasized *lot* with a broad sweep of his arm.

"I'd say sign me up, but I'm allergic to cow manure. And besides, what's the deal with overalls? Does anyone look good in them?"

Mason snorted, but a quick glance showed a smile on his face. "I might have rocked a pair of overalls in the past," he said.

"I'll believe it when I see the pics."

"Oh, I wore 'em. I may have been like three at the time, though."

"Is there anything you like to do besides wear overalls and mooch free rides from strangers?"

"I fix things."

"Like what?" asked Dee.

"Oh, anything."

"Anything?"

"Sure."

"My family?"

Dee couldn't believe she'd just said that, but Mason shrugged. "Get in line. I'm still working on my own."

"Ever fix a broken heart?"

"Have you got a broken heart?" he asked.

"Not yet," said Dee.

At that moment the truck's engine died.

They were just coming out of a curve and Dee struggled to straighten the wheel. She was going too fast to make the correction and the brakes were slushy. The truck's wheels slipped off the side of the road and a tree loomed in front of them. "Hold on!" she tried to shout, but it was already too late. She heard a loud crack and then darkness closed in.

*

When Dee woke up, she was lying across the bench seat of the truck and looking into a pair of dark, concerned eyes. She tried to sit up, but Mason held her down. "Just wait a minute. You practically took out the steering wheel with your forehead. I've got a first aid kit in my pack. I'll be right back."

Dee closed her eyes for a minute, and when she opened them again she felt a warm touch on her face. "Don't go to sleep, darlin'. Let's see how bad that cut is. This might sting a bit."

It did sting, but Dee kept her gaze steady on his face. Had he just called her *darling*? A lock of wavy hair fell over his forehead and he pushed it impatiently out of his eyes. It looked like he hadn't had a haircut in a while, but it added to his appeal.

She caught his wrist in her hand and felt the pulse beating quickly against her palm. He was wearing some kind of friendship bracelet, its colors bright against the dark tan of his skin.

"Good thing for me you like fixing things. Are you okay, though?" she asked.

"Don't worry about me. I've had worse."

"You've been in an accident before?"

Because he was leaning over her, looking directly into her eyes, she saw the change come over his features, turning his face cold.

"An accident." He snorted. "Yes, I've had a few accidents."

Dee didn't say anything else, and before long, Mason had her head bandaged and she was sitting up, looking around.

"I don't even have my license yet," she moaned. "My grandpa is going to kill me."

"Driving without a license? How old are you, anyway?"

Dee was fifteen. She didn't answer.

"Do you at least have a permit? Maybe he'll just maim you."

"Very funny." She looked out the window of the truck and blinked rapidly.

"Aw, I didn't mean to make you feel bad." Mason's voice was warm honey. "Listen, maybe it's not so bad. We haven't even tried to start it up again." He circled behind the truck to the driver's side and slid behind the wheel.

Dee wasn't surprised when he turned the key and the engine failed to turn over. She sighed heavily. "Look, I'm just going to call a tow truck. Hopefully my phone gets reception here. I think we're pretty close to town." She got out her phone to see if it had any bars. Strange, it was completely off. She hit the power button but nothing happened.

"Well, that's just great," she said. "The crash wrecked my phone. Looks like we're both going to be walking now."

"Mind if I look at the engine first? Sometimes it seems worse than it is. Like your forehead. Lots of blood, but just a tiny cut."

Mason popped the hood and started fiddling around inside. Dee climbed down out of the cab and made her way slowly around to the front of the truck. She inspected where she'd hit the tree and decided with some surprise that the truck had come out on top in that matchup. The grill was dented, but there wasn't any serious body damage.

Mason used a wrench and a pair of pliers he'd found in the vehicle's toolbox. The deft movements of his long fingers fascinated Dee as he checked over the engine.

She blushed when she realized she was staring at him and hadn't heard his question. "What did you say?" she asked.

He looked at her with concern. "Does your head hurt? I was asking whether you remember anything about the crash. It seemed like the engine just stalled out, but I don't remember you in the middle of shifting gears or anything."

"Gee, thanks for the strong vote of confidence in my driving," she snapped, more sharply than she'd intended.

"That's not what I mean. I just think it's pretty weird for a car to turn off for no reason, and I don't see anything in here that would have made it do that. I'm not saying it was your driving," he said quickly, catching the narrow-eyed look she angled at him. "It's just strange. Come on," he added, wiping his hands on his jeans. "Let's see if that worked."

Dee breathed an audible sigh of relief when the engine turned over and roared to life.

"That's what I thought," said Mason. "The impact just knocked a couple of things loose, but there wasn't any real damage." Then he looked at her with one eyebrow raised. "Are you going to be mad if I suggest you let me drive the rest of the way into town? There's a clinic in Lookout Falls where someone can take a look at that cut."

"Just so long as we're clear that you're driving because I'm injured, and not because I can't drive a stick."

"It's a deal," said Mason and held out his hand to shake.

His warm hand closed fully over hers, and she felt a shiver run through her. A feeling like that could be dangerous. Maybe her mom had been right about hitchhikers, after all.

CHAPTER THREE

When Dee's parents had driven her through Lookout Falls the day before, she'd gotten the impression of an older town where the residents didn't make enough money to pay for upgrades. She'd seen a couple of stores and a busy skate park near the community playground and pool, but for the most part, it was just dingy houses and a few traffic lights.

The sight that met her eyes when they got to Lookout Falls was completely different from what she'd seen yesterday. It was chaos. Cars were parked in the middle of the street and up on sidewalks with their doors left open. People were wandering around. Mason carefully steered his way through the obstacle course while Dee looked around anxiously.

"What in the world is wrong with everyone? Is it some kind of town festival?"

"If it is, they aren't looking very festive," said Mason drily.

They both watched as a mother unloaded five kids in wet swimsuits from a brand-new minivan parked in the middle of the road and told them to sit on the curb while she snapped a baby into a stroller.

"All right, troops," the mom ordered. "Form up—we are marching home. I'm going to have to call the tow truck from there." It struck Dee as ironic when she heard her remind the kids to look both ways before they crossed the street. The roads were full of cars but most of them weren't moving.

As they wound through town they noticed none of the stoplights were working and there were more accidents, including a couple that Mason had to backtrack to avoid. They saw a few other cars driving slowly through the maze, but most of the vehicles they spotted were stalled and left where they were.

"Maybe someone at the clinic will know what's going on," said Dee.

The scene there was worse. Every seat in the lobby was taken, and there were people sitting on the floor and leaning against the walls. Children cried and parents tried to comfort them while other people held bloody cloths to cuts or cradled injured limbs. A flashing yellow light on the wall indicated that the clinic was running on backup power.

Dee and Mason paused in the automatic doorway that was propped open with a wedge. As Dee took in the scene, her injury suddenly seemed extremely minor.

She saw a mother with a broken arm trying to calm a fussy baby. A man clutching his midsection snarled at her to keep the baby quiet.

"Can't you see there ain't nothin' she can do?" said another woman. "That baby's just sayin' what we're all feelin'. I never saw nothin' like that craziness out there. Every car dyin' at the same exact time, crashin' into each other."

The young mother wiped away tears and gave a grateful look to the woman who had come to her defense.

"It couldn't have been all at once," argued the man gruffly. "That wouldn't be possible."

"I know what I saw," retorted the woman. Dee saw several heads nodding in agreement.

Mason said quietly into her ear, "This might not have been the best idea. Let's get out of here."

Back in the truck, Mason switched on the radio and turned the old-fashioned knob all the way from one side of the tuner to the other. Nothing. They both sat and listened to the static until Mason reached over and turned off the radio.

At the motion, Dee's attention was caught again by the bracelet on his wrist. It was woven like a friendship bracelet but thicker, like a watchband. Mason noticed her curious gaze and said, "It's made out of paracord. You can unravel it in an emergency and use it as a rope."

Dee had never heard of paracord. She wondered if a girl had made it for him.

Mason interrupted her thoughts. "You should probably get back up to your grandfather's. I hear the train station is closed, anyway." He gave her hand a squeeze. At his touch, Dee felt her heart give a lurch.

"What about you?" she asked. "Maybe you could come with me."

He didn't seem to have heard her—he was distracted by something over her shoulder.

"What the . . ." he trailed off. She turned and saw huge puffs of black smoke billowing into the sky over the west side of town.

"Do you think it was a bomb?" he wondered aloud.

Both heads turned back toward the clinic when they heard the sound of a fire truck pulling out of the station next door. They watched as the truck tried to make its way down the street but was blocked almost immediately by cars that had been abandoned in the middle of the road.

"Come on," said Dee. "We've got to clear the street for them!"

The firefighters nodded to the kids gratefully as they started moving cars off to the side of the road. They quickly worked out a simple procedure: Mason drove the truck while she got into the cars. If the keys were in the ignition she tried the engine. About a third of the cars started, though their dashboard lights flickered or didn't turn on at all. She drove these to the side of the road. The rest she shifted into neutral and steered, while Mason pushed them aside with the truck. It was tedious, but the firefighters were working with them, and as people on the streets saw what they were doing, more of them started to help, too. The fire truck slowly made its way across town.

The two finally reached the source of the smoke and Dee saw that it was a power plant, one side already completely engulfed in flames.

"No wonder the clinic didn't have power," she murmured.

Mason and Dee watched as the firefighters leaped off the truck and uncoiled hoses. They got in position and shouted they were ready, but nothing happened.

"Come on, Tommy, get that pump on," one of the men yelled.

A voice from the top of the truck hollered down, "Can't get the valve open. It's not responding!"

The fire chief quickly scaled the truck to lend a hand, but the hoses remained limp and dry.

Dee looked the crew over. Most of them had patches on their shirts labeling them as volunteers. A few looked mature and experienced but a couple of them were probably only a few years older than she was. The crew gathered around the chief and Dee heard him say, "We're going to have to do this the hard way, folks. First priority is search and rescue. Matt, take your guys in over there and see who's left inside."

About half of the group wearing suits and masks ran into one of the side buildings. Smoke belched from a broken glass door, and now and then a human figure stumbled out.

"Everyone else be ready to support Matt." He gazed around the parking lot and quickly took in the scene. "We've got wounded. Get those people out of there and start triaging in the lot. No one goes near the main blaze." The rest of the crew started helping people off the grounds. Dee shuddered when a man with terrible burns and a mangled hand was carried past.

An out-of-shape middle-aged man ran up to the chief. He was wearing khakis, a polo shirt, a hard hat, and a thin layer of smoky grime. The fire chief apparently recognized him because he said, "You in charge of the shift today, Gene? What in the world happened?"

Gene shrugged helplessly. "I wish I knew. We lost power right around noon but the backups kicked in like they're supposed to. Next thing I know, one of my guys comes running in so freaked out he could barely talk. A bunch of them were on their lunch break out back. Say they saw the main transformer shooting sparks like the Fourth of July, right before an underground line exploded where it connected with the main plant.

"Someone pulled the fire alarm and we tried to call you, Max, but no one could get through. Landlines were all down, from the explosion, I reckon. Weird thing was all the cell phones were dead, too. Some kind of interference maybe, I don't know. I was sure glad to hear the sirens, though, I can tell you that."

"Wish we could've got here sooner, Gene. We didn't know about the fire until we saw the smoke." He paused and kicked the tire on one of the trucks. "This thing's useless, though. I always knew these trucks were getting too high-tech."

The fire chief continued. "I need you to go count your people, Gene. Tell me how many we're missing."

"We already did a preliminary count, Chief—that's what I was coming to tell you. I probably lost four in the first blast, but we evacuated the main plant pretty fast. There's still a few coming out of the business office, but I'd say we're about clear."

"Four? Are you sure?" The fire chief looked troubled.

A firefighter from the first group jogged over, his suit black and sooty. "Small building is clear, Chief."

"That's it then, Matt. Clear everyone back to the parking lot. We're going to have to let this thing burn itself out."

Another firefighter approached and reported, "We've got a few bad ones, sir. Think we should take them to the hospital in Louisville?" He paused. "I don't think the clinic is sending an ambulance."

The fire chief paused for a moment. "I doubt we can get the truck through to Louisville," he said. "Load 'em up and we'll take them to the clinic." He looked around the parking lot at people trying to start their cars and then pushed his hat back to scratch his head. "Heaven help us."

Dee and Mason offered to haul as many people into Lookout Falls as they could fit in the back of the truck with the tool chest. Pretty soon they had six people in back and an older woman in the front seat who said she was the receptionist. Dee let Mason drive again, and she sat next to him. Her head was pounding and she felt strangely heavy, like her bones had been filled with lead. The smell of smoke was thick in the cab of the truck even though they drove with the windows down. The receptionist stared out the window without speaking, but Dee could feel her trembling.

Mason drove slowly up and down the streets of Lookout Falls, trying to maneuver past the stalled and abandoned cars and take everyone home. They kept the window open between the cab and the back of the truck so he could get directions from their passengers. It was quiet otherwise, and Dee looked back once to see if everyone was okay. They were all holding hands.

She tried the radio again, hoping for some news or an emergency broadcast, but all she got was static.

Finally, they only had one passenger left, and he told them to take him to the east side of town. When they dropped him off, he came around to the cab and thanked them.

"Why don't you two come on in. You look beat."

Mason looked at Dee. "You wanna go in for a minute? I bet they've got some painkillers."

The man who'd introduced himself as Pete was momentarily distracted as three children launched themselves out of the house Tasmanian-Devil-style onto their father. A woman in her midthirties was right behind them, wiping her eyes on her sleeve.

"Thank heavens, Pete. I could see the smoke from here. Are you okay?"

Mason and Dee looked away awkwardly while Pete convinced his wife he was fine. After a minute he introduced them as "Mason and Dee—the kids who cleared the road for the fire trucks." Dee hadn't realized anyone but the firefighters knew about that. Next thing she knew, Pete's wife, Jennifer, had an arm around her and was leading her up the steps into the house.

It was warm inside but not uncomfortable, and they both sat in the west-facing living room, taking advantage of the slanting afternoon rays. Jennifer brought out bottles of water and ibuprofen for everyone, and then sent the kids to play in the backyard.

There was a brief moment of quiet, and Dee thought about her day so far—probably the strangest day of her life. She'd set off that morning half intending to be on a bus partway back to Columbia, Maryland, by now. Instead she'd picked up a hitchhiker and gotten in a wreck. Her parents were going to love that.

Then there'd been the fire at the plant. She could still hear the wounded crying in pain as they were loaded onto the fire truck and taken to the clinic. Now she was in a stranger's home, half listening and half dozing as he recounted his own day.

Jennifer interrupted him and Dee sat up with a start. "Listen, Pete, you know how I've talked about preparing for the end of the world, right? How we've been helping Mom and Dad stock the cabin?"

Pete, not catching her grim mood, shook his head at Dee and Mason. "You should see our bookshelves—full of books like *The Stand* and *Lucifer's Hammer.* You ever heard of that show *Doomsday Preppers*? I'm surprised they haven't made an episode about Jenn and her family."

"Will you shut up, Pete? This is serious. I know what happened."

"What's that, hon? That the plant burned down and the city lost power?"

"Stop being a jerk and I'll tell you *why* the power plant burned down. It was an EMP." Jennifer pronounced it "ee-em-pee."

Dee had never heard of it, but she saw Mason slowly nodding his head.

"I don't know enough to get technical," Mason said, "but I know it means electromagnetic pulse."

"Right," said Jennifer, "and everything that's going on here today makes me think that's what happened at noon. An EMP sends shock waves through the air at different frequencies. Some of the waves burn out electronics like phones and computers, and others at lower frequencies will knock out radio and telecommunications. The lowest frequencies send huge currents through power lines"—she said this pointedly to Pete—"causing overloads and fires."

"What causes an EMP?" Dee hoped it wasn't a stupid question. She felt like she was in science class and hadn't done the reading homework.

"There are a couple of things," said Jennifer. "A really big solar flare facing the earth can send a burst of energy our way that would hit us with the type of waves that damage power lines. Luckily, they don't travel at the speed of light, so scientists can see the solar flare ahead of time and give us enough time to prepare for it. Usually a couple of days. Power companies can shut down their grids to protect them from massive damage and outages.

"Some people are going to think that's what caused this, but they're wrong. Even a powerful solar flare wouldn't knock out cell phones or radio. No, to cause this much damage you need a nuke."

"As in a nuclear bomb?" Dee gasped.

Jennifer nodded. "I'm afraid so."

"No one would dare nuke the United States," said Pete, rolling his eyes. "We'd annihilate them."

"Not if they got in the first shot," said Jennifer. "It only takes one nuke to create an EMP that would affect at least half the country. The trick is to detonate it in space above us. It would explode so far away we wouldn't even see the blast, but the electromagnetic pulse it created would affect everything for hundreds, maybe even thousands, of miles.

"With just a few nukes someone could create an EMP attack that would take down all of the critical infrastructure in the country. Do you know what that means?" Jennifer didn't wait for an answer. "No electricity, for starters. No communications, either. That includes cell phones, radios, satellites. No Wi-Fi, that's for sure."

Dee reached into her pocket and felt her cell phone. Everything Jennifer was saying about the electricity and cell phones, even the radio, was pretty much spot-on. She shivered, though she wasn't cold.

Jennifer said, "We take the transportation network for granted. Besides rescue workers being unable to function efficiently, big rigs and trains won't be able to transport food. As a society we're used to going to the store almost every day to pick up what we need, but without regular shipments of stock arriving, the stores will be cleaned out in a matter of days. I expect the majority of people will start running out of food either this week or next.

"Water will be a serious issue around here within a few days, too. It takes electricity to treat and pressurize water for all the folks in town. Without it, how will they get clean water to drink? No one is going to have a flushing toilet after today, either."

"With no food or water people will be at each other's throats," said Mason.

"It's going to get really bad, and it's going to happen faster than you'd believe," agreed Jennifer. "I predict rioting and disease within the first week, and martial law and public executions before the end of the first month."

"Why do you have to be this way?" asked Pete. "You always blow things out of proportion. Rioting? Public executions? People are going to be upset about the losses at the plant, sure, but we'll get through it."

"You're not paying attention," said Jennifer. "This goes way beyond Lookout Falls. The plant here blew up because of a terrorist act that probably affected the entire Pacific Northwest, if not the whole country."

"Who could have done this?" asked Mason. "Russia? China?"

"I'd put my money on North Korea or someone in the Middle East," said Jennifer. "They might even be crazy enough to think they'll get away with it."

Dee tried to remember everything she knew about world politics, which was next to nothing. Why hadn't she paid more attention in current events class?

"So, are we at war?" she asked aloud.

Jennifer shrugged. "I don't know. Probably."

Dee struggled to take it all in. An EMP attack sounded like the plot of a low-budget sci-fi movie, not like something that could really happen.

Mason seemed to be having an easier time absorbing the information. "There are a lot of cars stalled out on the roads right now, but some of them still work. Do you know why?"

"I read a report not long ago that said an EMP could stall a car and burn out its electronics, but likely wouldn't damage every single one. It could be that the body of the car protects the engine. I don't know for sure."

"And planes?" asked Mason. His question caused an alarm bell to start ringing in Dee's head. She felt dizzy and clutched the arm of the chair for support.

Jennifer said, "Well, no one knows about planes. My bet is the pulse would stall their engines but they'd be okay if they could restart them. If not, they might just fall out of the sky. Either way, they'll have to set them down as soon as they can. Air traffic control and the FAA are required to have backup generators, but who knows if they're knocked out, or how long they'll last."

"And boats?" whispered Dee. "What about boats?"

"With boats it depends," said Jennifer, speaking more gently at the sight of Dee's stricken face, "but it might not be so bad. They don't need electricity to float, so they aren't in immediate danger. The bigger ones have backup power, too, so they'll probably aim for a port. The problem for them will be trying to get close enough to dock. My bet is passenger ships will have to unload via small boats, and cargo ships won't be able to unload at all. The cranes on the docks won't have power, so all that cargo is just going to sit in the boats and rot while people starve."

"Starve?" said Pete. "No one's going to starve. Everyone's just going to have to hunker down for a few weeks until the power companies can send in some crews to repair the lines."

"Listen," said Jennifer, "you saw what happened to the transformers today. Imagine all the transformers in the country blowing out like that. Without any power, how are we going to get them replaced?"

"Hey, this is America. We'll figure something out."

"Look at me, Pete." Jennifer put her hands on his cheeks and stared him in the face. "This is for real. In all likelihood, electricity and communications across the whole country are down. No one's coming to turn the power back on. People are going to starve, and they're going to get sick, and they're going to die. I need you to take this seriously. It's the big one. This is it."

Pete looked at her blankly. "What?"

"The apocalypse."

CHAPTER FOUR

Dee's mind whirled. Everything Jennifer was saying seemed like it made sense, but she didn't want to believe it. She didn't want the world to end while she was on a run-down farm and her mom and dad were out in the middle of the ocean.

"Are you guys sticking around?" said Mason to Jennifer.

"No, we're bugging out."

"We are?" said Pete.

Jennifer ignored him. "My parents live in a cabin a hundred or so miles away from here. We all help keep it stocked and ready. We just need to grab a few things and then we're out."

"Thanks for the water," said Mason. "And the medicine. They mean even more, now that we know. Do you have any advice for a couple of nonpreppers?"

Jennifer looked Mason up and down critically. "You might not be a prepper, but I recognize a survivor. You'll be okay. But I've got something for you just the same." She opened a file folder and shuffled through some papers. "Have you got any cash on you?"

"Actually, I do," said Dee, thinking of her bus money.

"Take this shopping list down to the Speedi-Mart and get everything on it you can. People are going to treat this like a regular power outage for now, so they're going to be buying short-term supplies like milk and bread. Those things will all go bad in a week, but the stuff on this list will keep for a while. You should be able to get a lot of it if you go now before people realize how serious things are."

"Thank you both," said Dee. "And if you ever need a vet, come find my grandpa. He's Milton Kerns, up north of town."

Pete nodded. "I'm sure we'll see you both again real soon."

Jennifer just shook her head and called the children in. "Who wants to go visit Grandma?"

*

Dee tried the radio in the truck again—static—while Mason drove them into downtown Lookout Falls. It wasn't much of a downtown, just a small market, a dollar store, and an antique shop. Down the street was a sporting goods shop.

Where were the stores? Did people really live like this? Townsfolk must do their shopping in Louisville. *Loo-iss-ville*, she mentally corrected herself.

"I think we should split up here, okay?" Mason's tone was casual. "I'm going to head over to the sporting goods store, and you cover the shops here." Dee wanted to argue, but Mason said, "It'll be more efficient this way. We can meet back at the truck when we're done."

"Okay," said Dee, "but you better not disappear on me. You're the only person I know in this town besides my grandpa."

Mason's eyes were bright on hers as he leaned closer. Dee thought for a moment that he was going to kiss her, but he just brushed her hair back and traced the line of her cheek. "Be safe," he said softly.

Inside the market it was crowded but strangely silent without the background sound of music. Dee heard angry words and turned to see what was going on. A man and a woman argued over the last case of bottled water.

Most of the people she saw moved purposefully through the store, loading up their carts with milk, bread, toilet paper, and other short-term essentials. Dee picked up a four-pack of toilet paper and then had to shoulder her way to the bakery. They were out of sliced bread, but they still had a couple bags of bagels, so she picked them up and went to look for a cart.

She was overwhelmed seeing how fast certain things were running out: fresh meat and produce, bread, milk and dairy products, junk food and soda. People weren't quite to the point of shoving or violence, but they were definitely snatching things up. She saw a woman juggling three gallons of milk run into a man who couldn't see around the four cases of water he could barely lift. The whole scene reminded her of shopping in Columbia, Maryland, before a big ice storm. Certain shelves would be completely cleaned out because people knew they could be trapped at home by ice and power outages.

She looked down at Jennifer's list. It didn't mention bread; flour was listed instead. That made sense—they could make their own bread. There were lots of bags of flour on the shelves, so she got ten pounds of white and ten pounds of wheat, plus a big bag of cornmeal. Her cart was instantly heavy. On the same aisle she got ten pounds of white sugar and a few bags of brown, along with a gallon of honey. Was she supposed to know what to do with this stuff?

Dee added salt, vinegar, baking soda, yeast, powdered milk, coffee, dried fruit and five big bags of pinto beans to her cart and then had to get in line to ring up because nothing else would fit, and even if something did, she doubted she could push the load. She kept a wary eye on the other customers, worried about what she'd do if someone tried to take her groceries.

A handwritten sign above the register announced, "Cash Only." She hoped she had enough from her bus money to cover the groceries.

The cashier was a young man about her age with sandy blond hair and a scatter of freckles that suited him. *Very boy next-door,* she thought. He looked flustered and distracted but he and the other cashiers were keeping the lines moving pretty well.

He looked over her purchases and sighed. "Do you remember how much any of this stuff was? The scanner is down and I can't remember the last time I rang up a super-size bag of beans. Also," he added with a grin, "I can tell you right now that you're going to hate yourself for buying twenty pounds of beans and no Beano."

Dee told him the prices as best she could remember, but in the end he was in a hurry and charged her much less than what she knew she owed him. It wasn't even half the cash she had.

"Listen, don't worry about it," he said. "At least you're trying to pay. I've seen a lot of people sneaking out with stuff under their jackets."

Dee thought about that as she unloaded her cart into the truck's storage box. Hopefully no one would try to rob her. She looked down the road toward the sporting goods shop, but there was no sign of Mason. His pack was still in the truck.

She still had plenty of cash so she went back into the store. She was surprised to see there were still quite a few of the items on her list on the shelves. There wasn't any peanut butter, but she loaded up on rice and olive oil before heading over to the canned goods. That section was pretty picked over. The corn and beans were mostly gone, and there wasn't a single can of soup or fruit. She sighed and picked up creamed corn, spinach, and asparagus.

Dee lucked out when she got to the canned meat section. Canned fish wasn't her favorite, but they still had some chicken.

She also tossed in tuna and salmon and some sardines for Grandpa. Old people liked kipper snacks, right?

There was room underneath the basket for two giant bags of dog food. They were so heavy she grunted as she loaded them onto her cart. Next she cruised the pharmacy area. There wasn't much left in the first-aid section but she found a box of Tylenol mixed in with the vitamins. There were plenty of those and she tossed some in the cart along with two crumpled boxes of children's Band-Aids and some shampoo and soap. She didn't spend time looking at what the options were—she just got whichever container looked the biggest.

Good thing Jennifer put tampons on the list. She never would have thought of those. Dee also tossed a bottle of Beano into the cart for fun, along with a case of European dark chocolate bars (all of the familiar candy was sold out), a crushed bag of chips, and a couple of premade sandwiches from the picked-over deli. She and Grandpa could have a picnic for dinner.

She noticed more and more people crowding the aisles and things starting to fly off the shelves. Dee quickened her pace. She had an epiphany and looked for the picnic aisle. She stocked up on paper plates, cups, and plastic silverware. Then she roamed the store, randomly adding, among other things, a pair of reading glasses, coloring books, playing cards, flip-flops, a package of socks, and twenty toothbrushes to her haul. She realized her heart was pounding and she was close to panic. Her cart was full and her choices didn't even make sense anymore. Time to go.

The line was slow and Dee could see through the large front windows of the store that it was getting dark outside. They'd have to close soon. Dee realized she had no idea what time it was. "Does anyone have the time?" she asked aloud.

"My phone's been dead all day," said a tired-looking man who smelled like smoke. He carried a basket full of first-aid supplies, and Dee wondered if he'd been at the power plant earlier. She brought a strand of her hair to her nose and sniffed. Yep, she smelled pretty bad, too.

"My phone's dead, too, and so is my MacBook," said a woman in slacks and a sweater set pushing a cart full of fresh fruit, cheeses, and artisan bread. "And I haven't worn a watch in ages. Does anyone know what's going on? I heard from a couple of firefighters that everything's down due to the fire at the plant, but that doesn't make sense. How could the fire fry my iPhone?"

An older woman with long, gray hair, thick glasses, and a cartful of charcoal briquettes said, "I read an article not long ago about how solar flares could cause power outages. That's what I think it was."

"Did it mention whether a solar flare could ruin phones and TVs, though?" asked the first man. "I haven't talked to a single person since noon who has a working phone, radio, or computer."

The older woman shrugged. "Your guess is as good as mine."

Dee thought about telling the others what Jennifer had said, but felt strangely reluctant. What if it caused a panic and people got hurt? Or maybe it wasn't true at all and Jennifer was just overreacting. Her own husband seemed to think so. The power could be back on tomorrow, for all she knew.

The older woman made eye contact with Dee and held up one hand while pointing to a plain wristwatch with the other. "It's almost seven."

Her grandpa must be getting worried and she still had a long drive ahead of her, maybe twelve miles. She also had to talk Mason into coming back to Grandpa's with her. She wondered why he hadn't come looking for her yet. Surely he had finished at the sporting goods store by now.

She dumped everything on the counter in front of the same sandy-haired cashier and saw that his tag said Hyrum. He laughed when he saw the jar of Beano. "This one's on the house," he said as she bagged it. Next he saw Dee's small pile of snacks and treats. "Party at the Kernses', eh?"

"How did you know I'm staying at the Kernses'?" Dee asked, eyes narrowed.

"Well, I saw you unload your first cartload into the back of Milton's old Chevrolet, so either you stole the truck and you're stocking up your hideout with"—he held up the canned fish—"kipper snacks or you're the granddaughter he told us was coming for a visit."

"Sardines are an excellent hideout food," Dee said with a straight face.

"I grabbed a few things for my family, too," he said. "Wish I'd thought of candy, though. My mom practically inhales chocolate when she's stressed."

He was adding up her total in his head. "You still have cash, right? Sorry I can't be exact, but it's the best I can do right now. I tried to give you a deal."

Dee picked up a calculator sitting next to the register and raised her eyebrows at him.

He shrugged. "Be my guest," he said.

She didn't even bother.

Unloading the cart into the truck for a second time, Dee wondered if she should have told the friendly cashier what Jennifer had said about the end of the world. He could get all the groceries his family needed and probably not even have to pay for them. They were all right there on the shelves. If Jennifer was right, who knew what would be left in a few days? Would any trucks still be making deliveries? Dee figured even if any of the trucks were still working, they probably couldn't get through the jammed-up roadways.

Dee looked around for Mason. He was nowhere to be seen, and now she noticed his backpack was gone, too. In its place was a sturdy new dark-green backpack, and when she unzipped it the first thing she saw was a note. She took it out with a trembling hand and opened it. By the last light of the sun she read:

Dear Dee,

Thanks for picking me up. I've got some things I need to take care of in town and I don't think your grandpa would appreciate another mouth to feed. Don't worry about me. I'll be fine.

There's something in the backpack for you. Have your grandpa teach you how to use it and keep it with you. Things are going to get bad, Dee. Stay safe.

Talk to you soon I hope,

Mason

P.S. Just think, it wasn't your fault you crashed the truck, after all!

Tears filled her eyes and Dee wiped angrily at them. Why was everyone in her life always leaving her? How dare he disappear? This was no time for playing the martyr. Dee tossed the note down and looked into the pack again.

He'd given her a gun.

CHAPTER FIVE

Holding the backpack away from her like it was a smelly diaper, she climbed into the truck and started the engine. After fiddling with various knobs and levers for five minutes, she resigned herself to the fact that the headlights were broken. Maybe they'd been damaged in the accident, or maybe by the EMP. Mason might have been able to fix them. *If he hadn't abandoned me, too*, thought Dee in self-pity. Now she was going to have to drive back to Grandpa's in the dark.

It was a long, tedious journey. The moon was up, but it was a thin, cold crescent whose dim light did little to illuminate the road. Dee finally got out and lashed a bright LED flashlight to the front of the truck. It helped some, though the light bounced alarmingly whenever she hit a bump.

Dee was surprised when she saw a country store with candles shining in the windows and a small group of people congregating outside. She wanted to stop and see what was going on, but she was too tired and just wanted to get home.

A mile or two past the store the engine gave a cough that made her heart sink. Next she felt the truck lurch and then sputter to a halt. None of the gauges on the dashboard had worked since the EMP, but she was sure it was out of gas. How was she supposed to get the food home now? None of the gas pumps in town worked without power.

Dee sighed and got out of the truck. She looked doubtfully at the backpack and then slung it over her shoulders and headed for home. Before she'd even gone two miles Dee was exhausted and thirsty and she regretted bringing the pack. The weight dragged at her shoulders and made her back ache. She'd trade it all for a bottle of water.

As she trudged up the road she saw a house through the gloom with a candle burning at every window. She could also see moonlight reflected in a little creek that ran through the yard. Though she knew better than to drink untreated water, she thought maybe a few sips wouldn't hurt.

As she got closer she realized she could hear voices through the thin walls of the humble house—the impatient voice of a mother dealing with tired, fussy children in the dark. "I don't know where the flashlight is," the mother insisted. "Last time I saw it you guys were using it in your fort. Did you bring it in?"

Dee couldn't hear the child's response, but the mother's next words were, "No, Daddy can't go get it. I told you, he's still on his trip and he won't be home tonight."

Dee's heart twisted in her chest. She knew exactly how it felt to wish your dad were there to step in and take care of things. Her pace slowed to a stop in front of the house as she thought of her dad and the many times he'd been gone when she needed him.

Next, Dee looked at the flashlight Mason had bought for her. She could manage without this one. With firm resolve she walked up the steps and then paused with her finger hovering over the doorbell of the small house. Would it work? Dee almost laughed at the absurdity of the entire day, and then felt a wave of anxiety.

She knocked. Instantly, the voices inside hushed and Dee saw little eyes peeking through the window. The door opened slightly and a young woman dressed in a Seahawks hoodie, with her hair in a messy ponytail, asked, "What do you want?"

Dee didn't really know how to answer, so she just held the flashlight out toward the door. "I could hear from the street that you don't have a flashlight. Take this one, I've got an extra."

The woman opened the door wider and took the flashlight. She turned it over in her hands and then passed it to her kids. In the gloom Dee saw the gleam of a flashlight shine on three small faces and heard giggles. The woman stepped out on the patio and looked at Dee searchingly. "Do I know you?"

"No, I'm staying with my grandpa, Milton Kerns, up north of here. My name's Madeleine, but friends call me Dee."

The woman thanked her and held out a hand to shake. "I'm Courtney. My husband would be here to thank you, too, but we're between jobs right now and he had an interview in Spokane today." Courtney looked toward the end of the street. "I actually expected him home by now."

Dee looked at Courtney in surprise and realized she probably had no idea about the situation in town or elsewhere. Not many cars drove by this way and Dee hadn't seen any abandoned vehicles for a couple of miles. Courtney had no reason to believe this was anything more than an electrical outage.

She was still talking. "My kids have been such a handful today. I didn't realize how much I take TV for granted." She looked at the children and sighed tiredly. "You think the power will be back on soon?"

Dee hated to give her the bad news, but someone had been kind enough to explain the worst-case scenario to her. She wanted to do the same for someone else.

As Dee told her what happened and speculated about what was to come, different worries chased each other across Courtney's face. Finally, she said, "You're saying it could be weeks with no power and no phones? With my husband stranded somewhere between here and Spokane?" Courtney's voice became shrill. "I don't even have two days of food here. We were hoping he'd get a job soon, so we didn't apply for food stamps or anything." Courtney's eyes were fearfully bright in her thin face. "I won't be able to feed my kids."

Dee looked at the three small children chasing the beam of the flashlight and felt sick. She could see that the family lived humbly. She imagined a lot of people here probably lived paycheck to paycheck. How many other families were in the same situation?

Dee looked at the youngest girl. She clung to her mom's leg and peeked out at Dee with one long-lashed eye. If Jennifer was right, this family might starve. Dee couldn't help everyone, but she could make a difference here.

"Listen," she said, taking out the rest of her money and pushing it into the woman's palm. "Take this and walk to the country store down the road. I'll watch your kids. Do you have a wheelbarrow or a wagon or something? You are going to buy all of the canned food they've got in that store. It doesn't matter if it's soup, tuna, SpaghettiOs, or Beanee Weenee. If it's in a can, you buy it. After that, buy out the energy bars. Get peanut butter and honey and crackers, and if they've got oatmeal, get that, too."

Courtney stood frozen on the porch, clutching the money and staring at her. "You have to go now," Dee said and gave her a little push.

The flashlight flickered across Courtney's face and Dee saw that her cheeks were wet with tears. "I can't take your money. You should get food for you and your grandpa. You don't even know me."

The two stood silent. Then Dee watched Courtney walk down the steps toward the store and tried to sort out her complicated feelings. She didn't know why she was helping this stranger, but there was something about the little girls that reminded her of her brother, and she knew she couldn't turn her back on them.

*

Dee considered herself an expert babysitter. When she was thirteen and too young to get an after-school job, she decided that she'd just as soon get paid to babysit other people's kids as babysit her younger brother for free. She took a class offered through the local community college, and when she found out she could charge higher rates if she was first-aid certified, she took that class, too.

After Jacob died she stopped babysitting. Little boys reminded her too much of her brother, and it was easier to stay in her room and avoid the world in general.

She could tell Courtney's kids wouldn't be any trouble. There were three little girls—at seven, Sarah was the oldest, Lexie was five, and Beth was three. The two youngest cried when they saw their mom leaving, but they cheered up quickly when Dee suggested a game of hide-and-seek. The people hiding all hid together, while the person who was "it" got to have the flashlight to find them. Dee might have been at a disadvantage since she'd never seen the layout of the house in the light, but the group of little girls gave themselves away with giggling every time it was her turn.

It was already late and she knew the girls were tired, so when she announced bedtime she expected them to put up a fuss. Instead, they each went to their drawers and started putting on their pajamas. Dee was amazed—she'd have to ask Courtney what her secret was. Even little Beth brought Dee a one-piece sleeper with feet, asking for help putting it on. While Dee got her dressed, Beth told her a made-up story about the three little kittens appliquéd on the fabric.

All three girls slept in the same room. Sarah and Lexie had twin beds and Beth was in a toddler bed. Dee was informed that each of the girls got to pick out one story for her to read to them, and they sat together on Sarah's bed while Dee read. When it was time to tuck them in, the two littlest ones wanted a kiss on their foreheads. Dee left the flashlight in the room and then went out to sit on the front steps and watch for Courtney.

She was used to seeing the orange glow of the city reflected in the sky at night, but here the sky was a black backdrop for a million tiny points of light. She'd never seen so many stars. Her mom had told her how in the summertime she used to sleep out in Grandpa's backyard in a sleeping bag on an old trampoline and fall asleep looking at the Milky Way.

Dee could see it now, too, a pale band sweeping across the sky. She wondered what her parents were doing right now. Were they looking at the night sky and thinking about her, too? She wondered if they had any idea what was going on here. Did they feel bad for leaving her at Grandpa's?

She refused to think that an EMP might have reached as far as their ship. If it had, they could be stranded in the middle of the ocean, and she couldn't handle that. She told herself that her parents would be back in a week or so. They'd see all the food Dee had squandered her life savings on and tease her about whether she was planning to cook it all by herself. Everything would be back to normal.

After a while Dee saw Courtney return, pushing the heaping wheelbarrow in front of her. Even though it was getting late, Dee stayed and helped her get everything up the steps and into the kitchen.

"How were the girls?" Courtney asked. "Thanks so much for watching them."

"They were great, perfect little angels," said Dee.

"Are you sure those were my kids you were watching?" asked Courtney with a laugh.

"Did you get everything you need?" asked Dee.

"And more. If we're careful we should be set for a few months. I don't know how to begin thanking you. You probably saved our lives." Courtney glanced toward the girls' room. "I don't know what I'd do without my girls. I don't think I'd make it."

Dee looked at the young mother's face and saw resolve. "You're going to be fine, and you can come up to my grandpa's farm if you need anything. It's about five miles up the road."

The woman smiled. "Apart from the store, I think that might make you our closest neighbor."

"Speaking of the store, how did it go?"

"You wouldn't believe what it was like there," Courtney told her. "It was insane."

"I saw a crowd when I drove by. Did you have to fight for the food?"

"No, that's what was so crazy. No one was buying food! Every last person in the store was buying booze, smokes, and girlie magazines. By the time I left they were sold out of all three."

Dee snorted. "I'm glad you've got your priorities straight."

CHAPTER SIX

As Dee neared her grandpa's farm, she could feel exhaustion etched in every muscle of her body. Jasper announced her arrival with a round of feverish barking, and when Grandpa opened the front door, holding a gas lantern and calling out, "Is that you, Maddie?" she stumbled into his arms and burst into tears. After everything that had happened to her that day, she didn't expect to hear herself say with a hiccup, "I wrecked your truck, Grandpa."

"Gracious, child, are you all right?" Grandpa held her at arm's length and inspected her. He even peeled back the bandage on her head to get a look at the wound. "Small and clean," he murmured to himself. "No need for stitches."

Dee was completely wrung out, physically and emotionally; she just stood in the entryway, hunched into herself. Grandpa considered her and finally said, "I can see you've got more to tell but it'll keep until tomorrow." He guided her over to the couch and tucked her under a thick blanket. "No need for crying now, Maddie-girl. You're home safe."

The soft couch enveloped her in comfort, and Dee felt herself drifting off almost immediately. One last thought winged through her head before sleep overtook her: *Am I really safe? Is anyone?*

She slept all through the day and into late afternoon, and when she woke up she was disoriented. She tried to remember where she was and why she'd slept in her clothes. As realization swept over her, she sighed and sat up. She knew she had a lot of explaining to do, but no idea where to start.

There was the EMP—an acronym for a technical term she no longer remembered and knew she couldn't define. Some kind of shock waves that knocked out the power and phones? Vague, but maybe it would do. Should she mention her parents? She didn't want to worry him with a lot of speculation, and she didn't want to make it more real by talking about it.

Somehow she needed to get gas to the truck, bring it home, and then find a place to store the bizarre assortment of food supplies she'd spent all her money on. Should she tell Grandpa about Mason? Admit that she'd picked up a drop-dead gorgeous hitchhiker and spent all day with him? And the gun—how was she supposed to explain that?

Dee's concerns were forgotten when she saw Grandpa come in from doing the evening chores. His face was a mottled gray and perspiration drenched his thin hair. His breathing was shallow and he couldn't quite seem to catch his breath.

She saw him stagger. "Grandpa!" she shouted and ran to him. Dee got him into his easy chair and put his feet up. How could she have been so stupid as to let the truck run out of gas? Now they were trapped here and her grandpa clearly needed medical attention. What if he died? She'd be completely alone. Just the thought of it made her dizzy.

She sat on the floor by his knee and held his hand until his face gradually regained its pink flush and his breathing returned to normal.

When he had his voice back he said, "Don't cry, Maddie-girl. I'm just fine. I haven't had an episode like that for a few years, though. Not since Doc Foster put that pacemaker in my chest."

Dee lifted her head from the arm of his chair and stared at Grandpa in horror. "You've got a pacemaker?"

"You look like you just swallowed a stack of lemons. And what's so bad about a pacemaker, I'd like to know. This little minicomputer in my chest is my own sweet miracle. I wouldn't be able to run the farm without it."

Dee swallowed hard. She hadn't wanted to believe what Jennifer had said about the EMP and the end of the world, but she had to face it. Now. Or Grandpa could die. She tried to make her voice sound steady. "It's a computer? What does it do in there, exactly?"

"Well, it keeps an eye on my heart and sends it a little shock if it gets to beatin' too slow. Before I got it I used to get episodes like this all the time. Instead of speeding up when I was working, my heart would slow down." Grandpa considered. "When the phone comes back up, I guess I'm going to need to call Doc Foster and get it checked out."

"About the phones," Dee began. "I don't think they'll be back up anytime soon." She told Grandpa everything about the day before, from when she picked up Mason all the way to helping Courtney get food for her kids. Afterward, Grandpa was quiet for a long time, and Dee wondered if she needed to try to explain again.

When he finally spoke, his first words surprised Dee. "You were right to help that young mom. I've seen her kids playin' out by their creek. It wouldn't be right to let 'em starve." Dee felt her throat clench when he went on to say, "I'm proud of you, Maddie. You helped the fire department, you showed compassion for a scared young mother, and you kept your head in an emergency." Then his eyebrows drew together and he said in a firm voice, "But if I ever hear about you picking up another hitchhiker, well, don't think you're too old to have your hide tanned."

Dee bit back a laugh. "Okay. But you'd like Mason. I couldn't have gotten through yesterday without him."

"He sounds like a fine young man, Maddie—but you *would* have gotten through it without him. You've got a strong spirit, and your folks taught you the difference between right and wrong. Don't you ever sell yourself short." He let that sink in for a moment and then said, "Now, we've got some plans to make, and I'd like to start by hearing what you've got in mind."

Dee sat up straighter. Grandpa trusted her, and he wanted to hear what she thought they should do. She took a deep breath to steady herself.

"First thing is to get the truck back up here. The problem is I don't see how I'm going to get gas. Do you think I could siphon some out of the tractor?"

Grandpa nodded. "I was thinking the same thing about the truck, but you won't have to get gas out of the tractor. How do you think I get the gas for the tractor in the first place? Can you imagine me driving it all the way in to town?" Dee shook her head, and Grandpa continued. "Back behind the barn I've got an aboveground gas tank that doesn't use electricity. You just open the valve and let gravity do the work for you. A lot of farmers around here have a gas tank."

Dee let out a long, relieved sigh. "And you've got a gas can?"

Grandpa smiled. "I've got at least three. Now what else do we need to be thinking about?"

"We need to take a food inventory, find a place to store it, and . . . Well, one of us needs to learn how to cook it. Also, how are we going to cook? Does the gas stove still work?"

"Excellent questions. We should check the stove to be sure, but the natural gas should still be in the lines, so I suspect it will work for a while yet. After that we'll need to think of something else."

"What about the woodstove? Isn't that what the pioneers used?"

Grandpa answered evenly. "I'd guess that might be dangerous for the oxen."

Dee realized he was teasing her. "I didn't mean while they were traveling!"

"Using the woodstove is a good thought, Maddie, but not in the summer. It will make the house too hot and use up firewood we'll need come winter. Let's save the cooking question for now. Anything else?"

Dee knew they needed to talk about the farm chores. She didn't even know exactly what they were, but figured they included feeding and milking the cows, taking care of the chickens, and tending the garden. Plus, whatever you did with crops in the fields. Now that Grandpa couldn't do any of that stuff—because of his pacemaker—it would all be up to her.

For a minute she wished she were back in Maryland with her friends. They weren't going to get pecked by chickens or have to pick acres worth of bug-infested corn. Even though she knew she was being selfish, she couldn't stop the wave of self-pity that washed over her. School was out and she was supposed to be having fun with Natalie, driving to the beach and hanging out at the mall. Not squeezing cow udders.

She played out the scene in her head. She was wearing pink boots and a cowboy hat, valiantly jumping between steaming piles of crap and trying to sneak up on a cow. The smell was appalling, and when she finally got close enough to touch it, the cow kicked her like a bucking bronco at a rodeo and ran to another part of the field. She was never going to be able to do farm work.

But if she didn't do it, Grandpa would, and that could kill him.

"Grandpa?" she said in a small voice. "I don't know anything about farming or animals."

"Come here, Maddie-girl," Grandpa said in a kind voice, and patted the arm of his chair. Dee sat close to him, and he put an arm around her waist. "I know this isn't going to be easy for you. Even if you'd grown up here on the farm, it would still be hard. There's a lot to learn and not much time. You're smart, though, and I know you're a hard worker. Together we are going to get through this."

Dee squared her shoulders. If Grandpa thought she could do this, then she would try.

*

Dee set out the next morning to get the truck. The worst part of the walk was lugging the gas can the whole distance. The fumes made her lightheaded, and it was heavy and awkward and kept banging into her leg.

When she got to Courtney's house, she saw the young mother out working in her yard while her kids played in a plastic sandbox shaped like a turtle. Courtney had a hoe and it looked like she was ripping out the shrubs and flower bushes that lined her yard.

"What's going on?" Dee called.

Courtney shaded her eyes and smiled when she saw Dee. "I found some old seeds in the garage and I'm going to plant them. I've just got to clear out some of these shrubs first and make room."

"That's a great idea," said Dee, thinking about her grandpa's garden. Some of his plants were already knee-high. "Isn't it a little late for planting, though?"

Courtney shrugged. "I've got to do something. Maybe I can cover them when it gets cold, or even bring them into the house. I already have a few potted tomatoes and herbs."

Dee said, "I wish I could stay and help—"

"You've already done enough," Courtney said firmly. "You gave me hope that my Rob is walking home from Spokane. When he gets here we'll raise a garden and take care of our kids. So don't worry about us. Not at all."

They chatted for a few more minutes about the kids, and then Dee resumed her walk. Apart from her grandpa's farm and Courtney's place, she hadn't seen any houses. The land on both sides of the road was hilly and undeveloped, used mostly for grazing animals. It was a gorgeous day but she didn't notice. She walked along the side of the road, kicking a rock with her sneaker, lost in thought.

Talking about Courtney's husband walking from Spokane made her think about her parents. She'd been dealing with one emergency after another and hadn't let herself consider their situation. Now, walking down a deserted country road, she couldn't think about anything else. Were they stranded in the middle of the ocean? Although she'd pretended to ignore them when they talked about their trip, she knew their itinerary by heart. Yesterday they were supposed to spend the whole day at sea. Maybe they hadn't been in range of the EMP. Even so, from what Jennifer had said it would still be a major obstacle for the ship to dock and unload its passengers.

Once her parents disembarked they'd be in a city where they had no family or friends, no food or supplies, and they'd have to travel more than three hundred and fifty miles, over the Cascade Mountains, to get to her. Even if their car still worked, they wouldn't be able to get it out of Seattle. Not when it practically took an army to get a fire truck across a small town.

Dee finally reached her grandfather's truck, and she climbed in and rested her head on the steering wheel while tears dropped down her cheeks. She'd been so awful to them this year. Dee had blamed her bad behavior on losing her brother, but hadn't they lost a son, too?

Had she even waved good-bye to them on Sunday? She knew she hadn't said a word.

Dee tried to pull herself together. She was wasting time. If Jennifer was right and this thing was as bad as she thought, Dee was going to be here for a while.

Just for a while. *"Don't say forever. Don't say forever,"* she told herself fiercely. *"They* are *coming back."*

Dee was wiping her eyes when she heard a sound she'd only heard on TV. When she turned her head, she was looking straight down the barrel of a gun.

CHAPTER SEVEN

The man holding the gun was in his midtwenties, with messy brown hair and hands that shook.

"Don't shoot," Dee said, putting her hands where he could see them.

"Does this thing work?" asked the man.

"Um . . . no?" Dee said, stalling, trying to think. She couldn't let him steal the truck. All of their food and supplies were locked in the cargo box in back.

"Get out," said the man, waving her aside with the barrel of the gun.

Her legs barely supported her as she opened the door and slid out. She was right next to the man, and his hands were shaking so hard she was afraid he was going to shoot her by accident. "Get over there," he said, pushing her roughly to one side.

Dee fell and the rough gravel bit into her palms. She pulled herself into a kneeling position and tried to think. Her heart was pounding out of her chest and she felt sick. How could she have been so careless? She had been so wrapped up in her own thoughts she hadn't even looked to see if anyone else was around. She'd been so busy feeling sorry for herself she wouldn't have noticed if he'd dropped out of the sky.

She looked around for someone to help her, but the area was deserted. Just open range and empty road.

There was no way she could let him take the truck. How could she stop him, though? A fifteen-year-old girl against a man with a gun? She looked over and saw he was already untwisting the lid to the gas tank, paying attention to something on the other side of the truck and not looking at her at all.

Dee reached into her pocket and carefully took the keys out. If she could just get the key to the cargo box off the ring, maybe he wouldn't try to get into it. There was no reason anyone should suspect the box was full of groceries.

Her palms were sweaty and they hurt from the fall, but she tried to hurry. *Which key was it?* There was the key to the truck and one to the house. There were a lot of other keys, too, and she had no idea which one it was. Maybe the one with *DiamondBack* stamped on it? She had to be sure.

The man lifted the heavy gas tank like it weighed nothing and began filling the tank. It took longer than she expected and she was grateful for the extra moments. Dee sidled closer to the truck, trying to get a look at the box.

"Stay back, girl," the man called over his shoulder. Dee froze.

He paused and then changed his mind. "Actually, I'm gonna need the truck key. Go put it on the driver's seat and then get out of here."

Key, repeated Dee to herself. *He said* key, *not . . . keys!* That was it. How could she be so oblivious? She took the truck key off the ring and slid the rest into her pocket. Her mind raced, trying to figure out how to get away safely and not let him take the truck. She approached the driver's side and thought maybe she could start it up and get away before he could shoot her. It had gas now, after all.

She knew it was hopeless, though. In the unlikely event she actually started the truck on her first try, she'd stall it for sure when she tried to leave. Then he'd shoot her. Maybe she could make a run for it with the key.

Dee carefully mimed dropping the key on the seat and stepped around the front of the truck, putting the vehicle between her and the man. She tensed her muscles to run.

As Dee came around the other side of the truck, she almost cried out in surprise when she found herself face-to-face with a woman. She was obviously pregnant and stood with one hand braced against the truck.

She was in labor, so involved in her pain that she didn't notice Dee at first, giving her a moment to study the woman. She was wearing a cheap knit tracksuit and her hair was pulled back in a scrunchie. Her bangs were wet with perspiration and stuck to her forehead as she panted in a quick rhythm.

Then she gave a low moan and the shallow breathing stopped, her entire body tensed. Dee held her breath without thinking about it. She gave an audible sigh of relief when the woman relaxed, her contraction over.

The sound alerted the woman to Dee's presence and she looked up quickly.

Dee held her hands out, skinned palms up. "No, it's okay, it's okay. I'm not going to hurt you."

The woman clutched the side of the truck and wiped a trickle of sweat from her cheek with the back of one hand. "My pains started yesterday. Tried to get to the clinic but the car's dead. Can't work the phone, either."

Dee considered. "I was at the clinic yesterday," she said, remembering the horrible scene in the lobby. "You might be better off at home. They don't have power and there were a lot of people waiting."

"It's gotta be the clinic," the woman said in a strained voice. "The baby's early and he's turned the wrong way. I can't . . . He's not gonna make it if we don't go."

Dee felt like time had stopped. She knew if she ran the man wouldn't chase her far. He couldn't leave his wife alone. Dee could get away. But if she ran away this woman and her baby would probably die.

She didn't even have to think about it. Dee wasn't about to leave her to die.

She opened the passenger door. "Come on, get in."

The woman pulled herself up into the passenger seat and sat there panting, lips slightly apart. Dee wished she had some water to give her, and wondered at herself, wanting to help the people who were stealing her truck.

Another contraction gripped her hard, and Dee shut the door. When it ended, she heard the woman whisper, "I'm sorry," through the open window.

Dee didn't answer. There were no words for this situation.

The man was done filling the tank and he slid behind the wheel. It was now or never. She showed him the key and said, "Can I at least ride with you?"

He pulled the gun out again. She thought he'd probably never pointed it at a person before today.

"Give me the key."

She wondered if he could really shoot her. His hand shook but the look in his eyes was steely.

Probably.

She handed him the key through the open passenger window.

"Once the baby's born and we get home, I'll bring back the truck. Up to Doc Kerns's place, right?"

Dee nodded.

"Honey?" The man used a different tone to address his wife. "It's gonna be okay. God sent us this truck so we could get you to town in time. Just hang on."

He closed his eyes as he put the key into the ignition. Dee saw his lips form a simple prayer of thanks as the engine roared to life. He put the truck into gear, and his eyes met hers as he turned toward town. There was no apology in them, just the desperate look of a man afraid for the lives of his wife and unborn child.

She watched as her food supply vanished down the road in a cloud of dust.

*

Dee's first reaction was to walk straight to the clinic and get the truck back. It was at least twelve miles, though, and she didn't think she could get there before dark. They desperately needed the food, but she needed her Grandpa alive even more. She was worried sick that he'd overdo it if she wasn't there to look after him. Without him, she knew she didn't stand a chance.

She hurried along the deserted road as quickly as she could, but a stitch in her side slowed her down. She hadn't planned on being gone so long, and in addition to her worry, she was hungry and thirsty now, too. Despite her attempt to speed her pace, the road seemed to stretch endlessly in front of her. Why did Grandpa have to live so far out of town?

A terrifying scene met her eyes when she finally got back to the farm. The cows had broken through a section of fence and were roaming freely in the road. Out in the pasture she heard Jasper barking and saw Grandpa's bent form.

"Grandpa!" she yelled, and ran toward him. She got there just as he collapsed to the ground.

"Oh no, no, no," she moaned and sank to her knees next to his still form. "Grandpa, you can't leave me. You're all I have." Dee felt panic rising at the thought of being alone. First her brother left, then her parents. Even Mason. But not Grandpa. She refused to let him go.

Dee turned him over and felt for a pulse. It had been over two years since she'd taken a basic first-aid class and at the time she was focused on learning how to help a choking child, not performing CPR. She frantically tried to remember what she knew about heart attacks.

There was no pulse in his neck or chest so Dee positioned her hands over his heart and began to pump. After a few compressions she remembered she was supposed to be counting. "One and two and three and four," she counted in a singsong rhythm. When she got to twenty-three she remembered she needed to give breaths, too. Not too late, she told herself and pinched his nose closed and breathed into his mouth. She distinctly remembered how the manikin's chest had moved with the breaths. Grandpa's hadn't. She knew there was a trick to it, but what was it?

Dee started the next set of compressions, counting aloud and thinking. "ABC," she said aloud, when it hit her. "Airway, breathing, and compressions." She tilted her grandpa's head back so his chin was pointing to the sky and tried the breathing again. This time his chest rose and fell with each breath.

"Come on, Grandpa, wake up." She shook him and yelled, "I need you, Grandpa, wake up." He didn't respond and she did another set of compressions and then listened for a heartbeat. She thought she heard a faint thumping. She checked the pulse point at his neck and it was definitely there—the beat was faint, but his heart was pumping.

Dee wanted nothing more than to put her head down on his chest and cry until someone came to take control of the situation. But no one was coming.

She looked around and spotted the cattle grazing on the long grass that grew in the roadside ditch. How she hated them. This whole mess was their stupid fault. If they hadn't knocked down the fence Grandpa wouldn't have gone after them and had a heart attack. It would serve them right if she left them out there and they got hit by a car. She giggled at the thought, and knew at once she was acting hysterically.

Dee needed to find a way to get Grandpa back to the house. An image popped into her head of a small trailer she'd seen in the barn. It was about the same size as a small wheelbarrow or large wagon, but it had a flat bed and she'd be able to pull it by hand. It might work but she was terrified to leave Grandpa in the field while she got it. What if the cows stampeded and trampled him?

She took deep breaths to calm herself down and felt Jasper's warm tongue on the back of her hand. The dog looked at her with dark brown, trusting eyes. His gaze assured her. He wagged his tail and looked at Grandpa. Of course! Jasper could stand watch. She told the dog to guard Grandpa while she went to the barn to get the trailer. When she came running back with it, she found Jasper sitting alert at Grandpa's feet and thumping his tail on the ground.

"Don't worry, Jasper, he's going to be okay," she said in a confident voice for the dog's benefit.

Still, she wished the canine could help her get Grandpa onto the trailer. He was solidly built and she could barely lift him. Finally she turned the trailer on its side and rolled him in over one of the low sides and then grunted and tugged at the cart until it was back on its wheels again with Grandpa safely inside.

Dee wheeled him straight into the house through the sliding door in the kitchen. It was easier getting him out of the trailer than in, and somehow she managed to get him up onto his bed. After a quick rest she took off his boots and socks, pants and shirts, and tucked him under the blankets, making him as comfortable as possible.

She checked his pulse again. Still there. Her lack of medical knowledge was frustrating—she didn't know what a good pulse felt like; she only knew that no pulse was bad. Not knowing what else to do for him, she kissed him gently on his wrinkled cheek and went to round up the cows. She might be a city girl, but even she knew that without the food in the truck, the cattle were the best chance they had to survive.

Once she had the animals in sight, Dee told Jasper, "Go get the cows, boy." Jasper knew exactly what he was supposed to do and started herding the cows toward her. *Bad idea*, she realized, too late. When she saw four twelve-hundred pound beasts closing in on her she screamed and ran. The commotion startled the cows, who turned and ran the opposite direction. Dee could have sworn Jasper gave her a reproving look before he went and gathered them up again.

This time Dee stayed near the fence, and once the cows were through the broken area, she wheeled the trailer in front of it. It wasn't a lasting fix, but it would do for the night. The little wheeled cart had proven it was worth its weight in gold.

Now that they were back where they belonged, the cows and the calf knew what they were doing. They headed for the barn, where Dee watched in amazement as the bull and two of the cows went straight into stalls. She hurried along and latched the gates behind them and then stared as they bellowed at her. It finally dawned on her when she saw the empty mangers that she needed to feed them, so she tossed some hay over the stall doors.

Jasper was facing off with the mother cow and her new calf. As Dee watched, she realized the dog was trying to split up mom and baby. He succeeded in herding the calf into a small pen alongside the cow's stall, but as soon as the mother bellowed, the calf came running out. Dee told Jasper, "And here I thought you could handle this on your own, dog."

Jasper gave a pointed wave of his tail as if to say, "I don't see you helping." Dee solved the problem by closing the gate to the calf's pen once the dog had it inside.

The mother cow was finally in her stall and it was the moment Dee had been dreading. She contemplated the milking stall.

"Am I seriously supposed to go into that tiny space with that huge cow? She'll crush me for sure."

Plastic bucket in hand, she tentatively approached the gate. When her hand touched the latch, the animal turned its head and looked back at her. Dee tried for a soothing voice, saying, "It's okay, I'm just going to milk you a little. Nothing to worry about." She sidled into the stall and put the bucket below the cow's udder.

"So far so good," she said to herself and reached for one of the teats. She gave it a pull and nothing happened. She pulled again and the cow stamped her back foot and snorted. Dee scrambled to get away from the cow and only succeeded in falling backward off the stool.

"It's not working," she told Jasper, who was watching from outside the stall. He wagged his tail. "Maybe the calf drank it all today." Dee hoped this might turn out to be the case, but knew it wasn't true when she looked at the cow's full udder.

"This shouldn't be so hard," Dee complained, and gave the teat a halfhearted squeeze. A little bit of milk dribbled out. Maybe you had to squeeze instead of pull. She gave another squeeze and a little pull at the same time and was rewarded when a nice stream of milk flowed into the bucket. "I did it," she shouted to Jasper. At the sound, the cow raised a back leg and calmly kicked over the bucket.

It took a while, and her hands ached, but Dee finally felt she'd gotten all of the milk into the bucket. She took it near the barn door where she could see it better in the fading light and was appalled—there was straw floating in the fresh milk. She picked it out with her fingers, pretty sure that wasn't the right way to do it, and then poured the milk into a clean glass bottle. One cow down, two to go.

Dee looked over at the pregnant cows and remembered how irritable her best friend's mom had been when she was pregnant. With that memory bright in her mind, Dee decided to let the expectant cattle have the night off. She checked the chickens' food and then considered the water situation. When she tried the hose nothing came out, and she didn't see anywhere to haul water from. Facing yet another unsolvable dilemma that night was too much for Dee. Exhaustion hit her like a fist to the gut and she didn't think she could have hauled water even if she knew where it was. The troughs weren't completely empty and she decided it would have to do.

She was sure she was forgetting a lot, but the animals were all in their own pens or stalls with food and some water, and she had a bottle of milk and three eggs. A warm feeling of pride filled her chest. She'd done the farm chores, and so what if it had taken her a few hours and a dog had done half the work? She'd never felt more capable.

The feeling of competence lasted until she went into the house to fry up the eggs and was faced with the gas stove. Dee was too tired to conquer any more unknowns, so she ate a whole jar of peaches from the pantry, checked on Grandpa, who was breathing steadily, and fell asleep on the sofa for the second night in a row.

CHAPTER EIGHT

When Dee woke up the next morning, she realized she was extremely hungry and thirsty. Her mouth was dry and her lips and skin felt thin and cracked. She thought back over the past couple of days and tried to remember when she'd last had a real drink of water. The previous night she had the peaches, which counted for something, but she'd barely had any water since the bottle at Jennifer's house. That had been Monday, and today was Thursday.

Dee knew her first priority had to be finding clean water, and wondered why she hadn't thought of it sooner. Most likely, she berated herself, it was because she took clean water for granted. At any given moment she was surrounded by sources of water—a fridge that dispensed water that had already been cleaned and filtered, bottled water, or worst case, tap water straight from the faucet or a drinking fountain. She didn't like the taste of plain water, often opting for flavored vitamin drinks or adding a drink mix to her water bottle.

This morning she'd give just about anything for a tall glass of water, no matter what it tasted like. She looked down at her clothes and realized she was still wearing the same thing from Monday. Ew. She was too thirsty to change, though, so brushed absentmindedly at the wrinkles and dust and thought through her priorities. First water, then the animals. She would figure out the rest later.

After she checked on Grandpa and changed the towels she'd put under him to try to keep the bed clean, she headed out to the barn. As she walked through the kitchen she noticed even Jasper's water dish was bone dry. Outside, the sun was shining bright, and Dee glared up at it. "I thought the Northwest was supposed to be rainy," she told the sky peevishly.

The animals were out of water now, as well, she noticed with concern. She hurried through the morning chores, milking the mother cow and attempting to milk the two pregnant cows. They weren't producing any milk, though, and even the mother only produced a scant amount. Dee eyed the fresh milk dubiously, but she was so thirsty she wasn't going to be picky this morning. After taking a small sip she licked her lips in surprise. The thick liquid coated the inside of her mouth with a creamy richness, entirely different from the thin, watery skim milk she was used to. It was kind of like a warmed-up milkshake. If she didn't think of it as milk it was pretty good. She drank most of the morning's milk and poured the rest into a small bowl for Jasper and the barn cats to fight over.

Her thirst partially quenched, she opened the doors of the barn and one by one let the animals out of their stalls, careful to stay well out of their path as they ambled out to graze. The thirsty animals went directly to a shallow, flat creek that crossed the lowest part of the property. Even the dog knew where to get a drink. Dee pumped her fist in the air when she saw water sparkling in the sunlight and hurried back to the barn for buckets.

Hauling water was backbreaking work and she had to make a lot of trips out to the stream and back. First she filled the watering troughs in the barn, and then she carried a full bucket into the kitchen. Even though she got the water from a relatively calm place, and she was careful to dip the bucket upstream from where the animals were drinking, silt had settled to the bottom of the bucket and there were leaves and dust floating in the liquid.

Dee poured the water through a coffee filter into a big pot and then contemplated the stove. This time there was no going back. She and Grandpa both needed clean water today and that meant boiling it.

On a normal gas stove she would turn the knob to "Light," hear some clicks, and the stove would light—just like magic. Unfortunately there was no fire or clicking when she pointed the knob of this stove to "Light." Worried by the strong smell of gas, she quickly turned the knob back off. She needed a way to make a fire. She looked around for matches and was rewarded when she found them in the first cupboard she tried.

Dee crossed her fingers and turned the stove knob again to "Light." Then she quickly lit a match and held it to the element, praying it wouldn't explode. Success! Blue flames circled the element, and she blew out the match and sighed in relief. Before long the water was boiling. Dee realized with a start she had no idea how long it needed to boil. She decided to just let it go for a while and hope for the best.

As she sat down at the table she was struck by just how little she knew. Her life up until now had not prepared her for a survival situation. She wondered how her friends in Maryland were dealing with the outages, and tried to imagine what she would have done if she'd been home when the power went out.

At noon on a Monday during the summer she probably would have been at the mall hanging out with her friends. They would have been annoyed when the power went out and unbearable when they discovered Sadie's car was dead and they had to walk home. Dee cringed as she thought about the number of accidents and congestion that would have been caused by all the cars and stoplights quitting at once in the relatively large city.

Once she finally got home, none of the appliances or the air conditioning would have worked—they were all electric. The house would have been terribly hot and humid. They did keep a decent supply of bottled water, but it would have lasted only a week or two, even with careful rationing. After that she didn't know what they'd do for water. Maybe try to find a creek and boil the water on the barbecue. But everyone knew the water was filthy and polluted, and the barbecue wouldn't have enough gas for more than a few pots' worth of water, anyway, especially if they used it for cooking, too. Not that there was much to cook. Her family ate out or ordered in most nights, so they didn't keep food staples in the house. Mainly just snacks and freezer meals.

Dee wondered how she would have handled it. Probably the same way she'd handled everything in the year since Jacob had died: by acting petulant and blaming everything on her parents, especially her mom.

The more Dee thought about it, the luckier she realized she was. In fact, her parents had most likely saved her life when they forced her to stay with Grandpa while they went on the cruise. She had done everything possible to change their minds and let her stay with her friend Natalie in Columbia. She'd tried slamming doors and refusing to speak, and gone to the other extreme of being helpful and friendly. Her mom had remained firm, and thanks to her, Dee now had fresh milk and eggs daily, and the possibility of meat. She had access to a garden, and if she didn't kill them (which was a possibility), she would have vegetables. The water situation wasn't ideal, but she had what she needed.

Their biggest problems, she reflected, were mainly her lack of skill and knowledge, and Grandpa's health situation. There was also the problem of the missing truck of food. Just the thought of all that food sitting down at the health clinic—if it was still there—made her want to tear her hair out, but she needed to take care of their immediate needs. Getting the truck and the food wasn't a priority, as much as she wanted to hike to town this minute and bring the truck home.

Dee scooped some of the water into a cup and let it cool before taking it in to her grandpa. He was in a slightly different position and she wondered if he'd awakened while she was out. She put a hand on his shoulder and shook him slightly. "Grandpa," she said softly. "Grandpa, wake up. I have some water for you."

He stirred slightly and opened his eyes. "Madeleine?" he whispered.

"It's me, Maddie," she said. "I just need you to have a little drink of this water." Despite all the challenges she faced, as Dee helped him sit up and take a few sips of water, she couldn't keep the smile off her face.

*

Days flew by as Dee cared for Grandpa and took care of the farm as best she could. She was busy from sunup to sundown, and grateful for the longer daylight hours. At night when it was finally dark and she could collapse into bed, she was already making to-do lists of the chores she'd been unable to finish during the day.

Hauling water took the largest portion of her time. Not only did the animals drink a lot during the hot summer nights, but she and Grandpa needed boiled water for drinking and cooking, and the large garden needed to be watered every day, too. They both watched the sky fervently for signs of rain. Grandpa had several fields of feed crops, mainly corn, wheat, and peas. Without electricity or water, the irrigation system was useless, and if the crops didn't get enough water the animals wouldn't have enough to eat in the winter. As if mocking them, the Washington summer seemed determined to make up for the previous wet winter. There wasn't a drop of rain.

Dee taught herself to muck the stalls after the animals went out to pasture, and she stopped being afraid of the cows and started being annoyed by their bad tempers. Grandpa said the two pregnant cows would deliver soon, so Dee had to keep a close eye on them. Supposedly they'd be able to deliver their calves by themselves pretty much, but they couldn't afford to lose a cow or a baby, so Grandpa insisted she tell him when they went into labor so he could monitor them.

He was recovering slowly and Dee tried to be patient. She wanted news of the outside world, but didn't dare leave Grandpa on his own. He had a TV that didn't work without electricity, and the one radio she found didn't have any batteries. Sometimes she wondered about possible war or invasion, but every day dawned much the same, and by nightfall she was too tired to do anything more than climb the stairs up to her room and fall into bed, exhausted.

Grandpa unearthed an old walking stick, which he used to hobble around the house. The handle was a clear crystal globe, and Dee thought it looked more like a wizard's staff than a farmer's cane. She pestered him with questions about where he'd gotten it, and he told a different, fantastical story each time she asked. Sometimes he teased her by chanting incantations and waving it over the stove while he cooked.

As soon as he could get around, Grandpa insisted on taking over meal prep. Dee sometimes wondered if her cooking had inspired his quick recovery. His first night out of bed had been the evening she'd attempted to make chicken noodle soup using boiled creek water, canned chicken, canned carrots, and some pasta.

Now they ate a lot of egg dishes, along with vegetables from the garden. Grandpa made a spinach quiche one day, which he said was easy enough but made Dee feel like she was back home eating at a French deli. They even had strawberries and fresh cream for dessert.

The thought triggered a sudden memory of middle school. She was having a rough time with friends and schoolwork. The girl she'd thought was her best friend had turned mean, spreading false rumors about Dee and making her life miserable. Dee's mom surprised her one day at lunch by picking her up from school and taking her to lunch at Le Madeleine. Afterward they'd blown off classes and work and gone shopping at the mall for the rest of the afternoon.

She wondered if she'd ever see her mom or dad again.

CHAPTER NINE

The days passed quickly, and Dee finally felt she was getting the hang of things. She knew she'd never been very good at hard work, but so far none of the animals had starved, and Grandpa was slowly regaining his strength, so maybe she was doing okay. She looked at herself in the mirror one afternoon after dinner and admired the arm muscles she was developing from hauling so much water. *Too bad about the farmer's tan, though*, she thought, rolling up her sleeves slightly and pursing her lips.

When she came downstairs Grandpa held out a basket and a fishing pole. "Take these and go on down to the creek. You've earned an afternoon off."

Dee opened her mouth to protest, but Grandpa raised a finger to shush her. "Don't think I can't see how hard this is for you, Maddie-girl. It just about kills me to have to sit and watch while you do all the heavy lifting around here. Even farmers take an afternoon off now and then, and you deserve it."

"Do you think it's safe?" Dee felt a pang of fear remembering the man who'd stolen the truck and pointed a gun at her. Maybe she should be carrying the gun Mason gave her, but she didn't know how to use it, and hadn't she read once that a criminal was likely to use someone's own gun against them?

"Sure it's safe. It's not that far. Practically shouting distance. Besides, did you know we missed the Fourth of July? It was last week."

Dee realized she didn't even know what day of the week it was. The animals didn't eat less (*or poop less,* she thought to herself) just because it was the weekend. Grandpa gave her directions to his favorite fishing hole, and Dee found herself walking down the lane with a basket of leftover fried chicken and what might possibly be the last can of Coke in the world.

While she walked she thought about Mason and wondered what he was doing. Probably eating power bars and living like a hermit in the woods. She wasn't mad at him anymore or holding a grudge. He probably left because he hadn't wanted her cramping his style and didn't know a nice way to tell her. It was too bad, though; they could have used another pair of hands on the farm.

The trail meandered through the woods, and dappled sunlight cheerfully danced between the trees. A cluster of purple wildflowers reminded Dee of her mom.

Dee could hear the rushing of the creek before she could see it and wondered if it really had fish. She hadn't had the heart to tell Grandpa she'd never been fishing and didn't have the first idea how to do it. Her plan was to find a pleasant spot to spread her blanket and then read for a while or take a nap. It was supposed to be a holiday, after all, right? She could learn to fish another day.

Dee stepped into a clearing and stopped short, heart in her throat. It seemed someone else knew about Grandpa's favorite fishing hole. The fisherman had his back to her and for a fleeting moment she hoped it was Mason. Then the sun flashed on sandy blond hair and she decided her best bet was to sneak away before he noticed her. There was no telling how he might react, and despite

Grandpa's assurance that they were in shouting distance, Dee knew no one would hear her if she screamed.

Too late—the blond head swung around and Dee met a pair of familiar blue eyes.

It was Hyrum, the checkout boy from the grocery store in town. He was wearing jeans and a somewhat ragged but clean T-shirt that said, "I'M YOUR DENSITY." He flashed a friendly smile at her and said, "Doc Kerns's granddaughter, right? My mom's been wondering how you folks are getting along."

Dee's fear was instantly replaced by the wish that she'd taken the time to brush her hair before she'd left the house. She was aware that her clothes were grubby and, never mind a manicure, she hadn't even been able to *clean* her fingernails properly in weeks.

"We're okay, I guess," Dee said, tucking her free hand into her pocket. "How's the fishing?"

"Lousy. It's the wrong time of day for it," said Hyrum. "I really just wanted an excuse to get out of the house. I've got two younger brothers and a little sister and some days I need a break. Don't get me wrong. I love 'em and all, but sometimes it's nice to be alone."

Dee took a step back. "I'll let you be alone, then. I don't really know how to fish anyway."

"No, no, that's okay. That's not what I meant. You should stay." He spied the book under her arm. "Whatcha reading? Anything good?"

Dee blushed and showed him. It was another Louis L'Amour book. Although she'd wished several times that her grandpa had broader taste in books, she still found herself enjoying his collection of Westerns. She was working her way through a series about a family who migrated from England and settled in the Appalachian Mountains. She loved the way they stuck together through good times and bad.

Hyrum nodded. "Who's your favorite Sackett? Mine's Jubal."

Before she knew it, Dee and Hyrum were sitting together on her blanket discussing books and music. When Dee offered to share her picnic, Hyrum pulled a square wrapped bundle out of his bag and handed it to her. "It's just some bread, but Mom made it this morning and it's really good." Dee couldn't take her eyes off the bread, so she didn't notice when Hyrum saw the fried chicken, until he gave a shout that practically scared her out of her skin.

"You have fried chicken? Oh man, I can't take that. I mean, bread is good but that would be taking advantage of you."

"Are you kidding?" said Dee incredulously. "I haven't had bread for weeks. I'm the one getting a deal here." She held the fresh bread up to her face and breathed in the comforting aroma of yeast and security.

They finally split up their picnic evenly, and Hyrum faked a swoon when he saw the can of Coke. "You must be some kind of angel, you know that?" he said and took a swallow. "We have food stocked up at home, but no pop. Next time the apocalypse hits remind me to buy chips and gum."

Dee thought of the gum in her pocket and contemplated kissing Hyrum. He was undeniably attractive, with his blond hair cut neatly and his tall, solid build. He even had a dimple when he smiled, but he didn't seem like the kind of guy you just kissed for fun.

Hyrum hadn't noticed her studying him. He was too intent on the fried chicken. "That was better than KFC." He glanced at her and switched to a Scottish brogue. "I hate the Colonel, with his wee beady eyes."

Dee was confused. Was she supposed to know what he was talking about?

He went on in the terrible accent. "He puts an addictive chemical in his chicken that makes y'crave it fortnightly!" Then he shouted "Coo-coo!" and started to laugh. Dee had no idea what was going on, but it felt good to laugh with a friend. She hadn't realized how much she'd missed that.

"Want to see something scary?" he asked when they'd finished eating.

"I don't know," said Dee. "Like dead-bodies scary? Demon-house scary?"

"Not that bad. More like wild-animal scary." He bent his fingers into a claw hand and raked the air.

"If it's not too far. I've got to get back soon."

"I'll get you home before curfew, don't worry," he teased.

While they walked, she told him about Grandpa's trouble with his pacemaker, and he told her he had an older brother who was stuck in California when the EMP hit.

"So you think it was an EMP?" she asked him.

"For sure." He held a branch so it wouldn't snap back at her. "Some military guys came into the store the second or third day and told me about it. At first I thought they were exaggerating or showing off. They were practically, like, 'That's it, game over, man. Game over,' but now I think they were right. Mom and I have been talking about it, and we think things are going to get really bad before they get better."

"Do you think it's true? That someone set off a nuke over the US?"

Hyrum shrugged. "I dunno, maybe. What do you think?"

"If they did, we could be at war right now and not even know it. Do you ever wonder what's going on out there?"

"All the time, Dee." He put out a hand to stop her. "Look over there. See that cave?"

Dee looked and saw a hole in a rocky outcrop. Balanced precariously above the hole was a fallen tree that looked like it would come down with just a breath of wind.

"My dad used to bring us out here and tell us stories about that cave. He said when he was a boy there was a family of bears that lived in the area and hibernated in the cave."

"Are there bears around here?" Dee asked, looking around nervously.

"One night on a scout trip I thought I heard a bear outside my tent. I had all my candy in the tent even though the scoutmaster told us we were supposed to lock it all up for the night. You know bears can smell treats, right? Even if they're wrapped up."

Dee wondered if a bear could smell the gum in her pocket. "What happened? Did it try to get in?"

"I ate candy until I got sick and then tossed the rest across the tent to where my friend was sleeping. We both survived the night, but I didn't have any candy for the rest of the trip." Hyrum grinned and his dimple was adorable. Dee thought he was sweet. She felt comfortable around him, but not exhilarated the way she'd felt when she was with Mason.

Hyrum squinted at the sun. "We'd better get going. I'll walk you back to the road."

Dee followed, but she gave the bear cave a long last look over her shoulder. She didn't think she'd be making any more solo fishing trips.

*

The next morning, as Dee hauled endless buckets of water to the garden with the trailer, she saw two people walking down the lane from the road. She left the trailer in the field and ran back to the house.

"Someone's coming!" she said, bursting in to warn Grandpa, but Jasper had beaten her to it. Grandpa was already watching out the front window. He had a shotgun.

"Lock the door, Maddie," was all he said.

As the couple drew closer, Dee realized it was Hyrum. With him was a middle-aged woman, and as Dee looked more closely she saw that it wasn't two people, but three. A little girl walked between them, holding their hands, and Hyrum and the woman swung her into the air every few steps.

Grandpa put down the shotgun and said, "Looks like you're about to meet the neighbors."

*

Everyone sat out on the porch, and Grandpa offered cups of the water Dee had boiled that morning.

"It's kind of you to offer us anything. Thank you," said the woman. "We've brought something for you, too." She handed Grandpa a covered dish, and when he opened it Dee's mouth watered as she saw no-bake chocolate cookies.

She glanced pointedly at Hyrum, remembering his comment in the store about his mom craving chocolate when she was stressed. Hyrum's eyes were merry as he silently put a finger to his lips.

The woman introduced herself to Dee as Angela Searle. "This is my son Hyrum, who you've met, and my daughter, Katy. I've got two more boys back at home and another who was in California, last we heard."

Angela shook Dee's hand firmly, and Katy gave her a high five and then giggled. She couldn't have been older than five, and Dee watched as she worked up the courage to pet Jasper, who had his mouth open in a panting dog smile as he watched the child approach.

"We haven't seen your truck around lately, Mr. Kerns. You having trouble with it?"

"Bad business with the truck," Grandpa said. "A man took it from Maddie at gunpoint last week. He had an ailing wife, but that weren't no reason. He could've asked for a ride instead of stealing it."

Hyrum nodded. "You should see how it is down in Lookout Falls."

"Pretty bad?" asked Grandpa.

"And getting worse," said Hyrum. "The stores were cleaned out of food and water in less than a week. Turns out your granddaughter did her shopping just in time. By Tuesday afternoon we had people walking the aisles with big trash bags, filling them with anything they could get their hands on and walking out with it."

"Why didn't you lock the doors and keep it for yourselves?" Dee asked curiously.

"We've got some food put away," said Hyrum.

"But there might not be more food shipments for months," Dee insisted. "Aren't you worried you'll run out?" She was imagining having access to a whole store of food and letting people loot it while her family went hungry.

"They're Mormons," said Grandpa, as if that explained everything.

It meant nothing to Dee, though. She didn't think Mormons ate less than other people. All she knew about them was their habit of knocking on her door at the worst possible times and biking in the most inappropriate clothes. "So you're going to go door-to-door for food?" she joked.

Hyrum laughed. "No, we just like to be prepared."

Dee decided she liked the way his eyes crinkled at the corners when he laughed, as if he did it a lot.

In the silence that followed, Angela looked at Grandpa and said, "We've known each other for what, ten years?"

Grandpa nodded. "You're good folks. I couldn't ask for better neighbors. It was a real shame about your husband."

"Thank you," said Angela. "You've been a good neighbor to us, too."

She glanced at her little girl, who was having her face washed thoroughly by Jasper, and then looked back at Grandpa.

"Hyrum and I have been talking about what it's going to take to survive the next year. We don't think the government is going to have the power back on for everyone for at least that long. Probably longer for us country folks. We think people will have a better chance if they work together, and we want to see if you'd like to work out some kind of agreement with us."

Grandpa rubbed the crystal ball on his cane thoughtfully, as if trying to see into the future. "What do you propose?"

Hyrum spoke up. "My brothers and I are hard workers. You've got all this farmland but not enough people or equipment to work it. We'll help you with your land and animals for the summer."

"In exchange for fresh milk every day and some young chickens to start our own flock," said Angela.

Grandpa nodded slowly, thinking it over. "It sounds like you've given this some thought."

"We think it would be a good arrangement for both our families," said Angela.

"I agree," said Grandpa, "and I'd like to propose a few other things. In addition to helping us with farm chores, we could really use help putting up wood for the winter. Do you trust any of your boys with an axe?"

"Absolutely," said Angela. "Hyrum and Jeremiah both have plenty of experience chopping wood, but we don't need a separate agreement for that. My boys will help you with any jobs you have here."

"Won't you need them at home?" asked Dee.

"I will, so let's say they'll be here every morning from just after breakfast until dinnertime."

Dee was finally accustomed to dinner being the afternoon meal, and she nodded sagely at the reference.

Grandpa spoke up. "As much as I could use the help, I'm not sure that's a fair deal for you. Milk and chickens don't seem like much in exchange for a full summer's work."

"One of these days I imagine you'll have people lining up to work for you in exchange for less. Fresh food is already a luxury," answered Angela.

"We haven't talked about harvest yet," Grandpa pointed out. "Once the fields start to come on, I could use your boys' help all day."

"We thought of that, too," she said, with a glance at Hyrum. "In exchange for unlimited help during the harvest, we would like ownership of one of this year's calves. A female, and we'd like to keep her here on the farm until she's ready to wean."

"And eventually breed her to your bull," added Hyrum.

"Now that's a tall order," said Grandpa, steepling his fingers, "but I think we might be willing to do that, if you're willing to throw in canning and cooking lessons for Maddie here."

Dee's cheeks flushed. "I don't need cooking lessons," she protested.

"You've got a deal," said Angela, rising to shake Grandpa's hand. "Though I feel like we're taking advantage of you."

"Oh, believe me," Grandpa said, carefully not looking at Dee, "we're getting the better end of this deal."

CHAPTER TEN

Having the Searle boys around to help with the chores was a huge improvement. Dee started each morning early with a cup of hot milk (the coffee was long gone and it was one of the few staples the Searles didn't have) and a few minutes of discussion with Grandpa about the priorities for the day. When Hyrum, Jeremiah, and the youngest brother, Joseph, arrived, they handled the more labor-intensive chores like hauling water and mucking out the stable. With slightly more time on her hands, Dee was able to spend more time in the garden, which she enjoyed.

A couple days into the new arrangement she saw Hyrum heading for the barn. He waved at her. "It's four thirty. Time for milking." He spoke with a strange accent, German maybe. And it wasn't four thirty. It was more like eight or nine in the morning. Dee shook her head. He had a weird habit of quoting old '80s movies. She'd learned that when he said something really strange it was probably a reference to a movie she hadn't seen and—came the unbidden thought—might never see.

When he came out a while later he walked over to where she was weeding tomato plants. It was close to noon, and his shadow pooled darkly around his feet. “My mom sent you a treat,” he said, handing her a brown paper lunch bag.

She looked inside and caught a whiff of cinnamon and spices. “No way,” she said, shading her eyes to look at him. “Is that what I think it is?”

“Yes way,” said Hyrum with a grin.

“I can’t take that. It could be the last banana bread in the county. Maybe even the state.”

Even as she spoke she unwrapped the morsel. She bit into the moist, cake-like treat and closed her eyes. After weeks of a virtually no-carb diet, the bread was pure bliss.

“Wait ’til you taste her zucchini bread,” Hyrum said mysteriously.

“Ew! Seriously? Zucchini-flavored bread?” Dee wrinkled her nose. “I’ll pass. I can wait for them to start shipping bananas again.”

“Trust me. You’ll change your mind when you try it.” He gave a pointed look at the piece of bread in her hand.

“Nu-uh,” said Dee, inspecting the bread for signs of unwanted vegetables. A few slivers of green caught her eye and she decided maybe she was better off not knowing. She took another bite and asked, “Why is she baking, anyway? Doesn’t it use a lot of gas?”

“Have you ever heard of a solar oven?” Dee shook her head, and he continued, “It’s basically a box lined with tinfoil. You put it outside on a sunny day and the sun heats the inside of the box. You can even hard-boil eggs with no water.”

The conversation was veering too close to cooking lessons for Dee’s comfort. As far as she was concerned, she and Grandpa could keep eating scrambled eggs.

She changed the subject. “I’ve been thinking if one of you wouldn’t mind staying with Grandpa, I’d go into town and see if the truck is still at the clinic.”

“Kind of a slim chance, don’t you think?”

Dee didn't want to hear that. She shrugged. "I still want to check."

Hyrum nodded. "Jeremiah will stay with your grandpa. I'll send him over after dinner."

*

Dinner was a spinach salad topped with a boiled egg and the last can of tuna. *Not bad for apocalypse food,* thought Dee. The pantry shelves were starting to look empty, though. There hadn't been much there in the beginning, and without the garden and the chickens she knew they'd probably be out of food by now.

"Maddie." Grandpa rested a worn hand on her arm. Dee looked up from her empty plate and saw his eyebrows knit together with worry. "I shouldn't let you go. We can get by without the truck and the food."

"It'll be okay, Grandpa. I won't go far into town, just enough to see if the truck's at the clinic. If it's not I'll turn around and come straight back."

Grandpa shook his head. "I wish I could go with you."

"I'll go with her, sir." At the sound of the voice both Grandpa and Dee started in surprise. Jeremiah and Hyrum stood in the doorway. Hyrum continued, "I brought a couple of bikes so we can get there and back before dark."

"God bless you, son," said Grandpa. "Keep her safe. She's all I have left."

*

It was an ideal afternoon for a bike ride, and Dee was slightly surprised when she realized she was enjoying herself. She hadn't thought she'd ever look at a bike again, let alone ride one. But the road to town was beautiful and Hyrum was good company.

"So how'd you get your nickname?"

Dee was relaxed in the warm summer sunshine as they cruised the empty road, and she heard herself answer. "When my brother Jacob was really little, just learning how to talk, he couldn't say 'Maddie,' so he said 'Dee.' It kind of stuck."

"I didn't even know you had a brother. Is he with your folks?"

"I wish. He died about a year ago." Dee was surprised she'd been able to say it out loud. She never talked about it. Tried never to think about it.

"That's awful," said Hyrum, and the sympathy in his voice made tears spring to her eyes. She blinked quickly and the wind caught and blew them away.

"I bet you miss him," Hyrum said.

"Like crazy, every day." Her voice came out gritty and rough.

"What happened?"

She'd never told anyone the story. She'd refused to go to the group therapy her parents had tried to talk her into, and her friends had all known better than to bring it up around her.

Dee's hands tightened on the handlebars, and she forced herself to speak. "He was riding his bike to meet me at my school. We used to ride home together every day after class. It's a big road, like three lanes, but there's a bike lane, too. Lots of kids ride on that road; there's a school speed limit and everything. But on that day, some guy was in a hurry to get to the high school and he used the bike lane as a turning lane.

"Someone who saw it said the guy didn't even check to see if it was clear. He just flew over into the lane and hit my brother's bike from behind." Dee paused for a minute. The next part was the hardest for her. It was the part that kept her awake at night and made her throat clench tight every time she thought of it. She made herself go on. "I know he was alive for a few minutes, afterward. No one in my family got there in time. No one told him good-bye. I wasn't even that far away, just down the road at the school messing around with my friends. I was so stupid."

Hyrum was quiet. Even the birds seemed to have stopped chirping. The only sound was the whoosh of their tires on the road and the wind in her ears.

"I never got to say good-bye," said Dee in a small voice.

"I've wondered which is worse," said Hyrum. "My dad fought cancer for two years before he died. Sometimes toward the end it felt like I was saying good-bye to him every day. I feel selfish now, especially after hearing about your brother, but at the time I thought it would be better if he went quick, without suffering. I didn't think I could watch my mom or my dad go through another day."

Dee could hear her own sorrow reflected in Hyrum's voice, but angry words still bubbled out of her. "How can you say that? Don't you know how lucky you are? I missed my last chance to ever talk to my brother. He's gone now, and he spent his final moments surrounded by strangers. He was alone, and now he's gone. How can that be better?"

Hyrum was quiet for a long time, and Dee almost regretted her harsh tone. Finally he motioned her to stop, and they pulled their bikes to the side of the road. Hyrum laid down his bike and wrapped his arms around Dee.

Dee wanted to push him away, to say she was fine. But she felt safe with him—as though his strong arms could block out her imagination and her loneliness.

Finally he let her go and looked searchingly at her face. "Can I tell you something? It's what I think about when I'm missing my dad the most. I know that someday I'll see him again after I die."

Dee shook her head. "Seriously? I mean, good for you, but I gave up on all that a long time ago. Heaven is a nice idea for other people, but I don't buy it. When we die, that's it. Game over."

Hyrum's eyes were sad. "You must feel so alone," he said. "Would it be worth trying to believe, if it gave you hope you'd see your brother again? Not even believing, but just hoping?"

She shrugged. "There's no way to be sure, so what's the point?"

"Getting a chance to tell your brother you love him. To hug him and tell him it'll all be okay. That's the point."

Dee felt her throat tighten and her chest tingle. For a moment she wondered how it would be to believe her brother was in a better place somewhere, waiting for her, instead of decomposing in a coffin six feet underground.

Even as part of her dared to hope, she felt doubts creeping in. Believing in heaven meant believing in God, and if there was a God, why had he let the world get so screwed up? Believing in a God like that was worse than not believing at all.

She pushed Hyrum away. "We need to get going," she said tightly.

"All right, but I'm here, any time you want to talk."

Dee was done talking. She kicked off hard from the pavement and coasted down the road alone.

CHAPTER ELEVEN

As they rounded the curve that would take them into town, Dee and Hyrum slowed their bikes to a halt. A fire truck and a few other vehicles were parked across the roadway to form a barrier. The ladder of the truck was fully extended and a woman with a rifle was up in the bucket about sixty feet over their heads.

"Dang," muttered Hyrum, tilting his head back.

A man came around from behind the barrier and looked them over. Then he pointed back the way they'd come. "You kids need to get back on your bikes and go on home. There ain't no reason for you to come into town."

Dee said, "We're not going to stay. My grandpa's truck was stolen and we came to get it back."

The man crossed his arms over his chest. "I don't think so. No one goes into town. No exceptions."

Hyrum spoke up. "Aw, come on, Matt, you know me. It's Hyrum Searle and this is Milton Kerns's granddaughter. We're not here to cause trouble, we just need to get Doc Kerns his truck back."

The man shook his head and said, "Rules is rules."

Dee remembered him now. He was one of the firefighters she'd seen at the power plant. She tried desperately to think of a way to change his mind. Then it hit her. "You know me! Do you remember when I helped clear the road for the fire trucks? The day the power went out?"

Matt nodded. "I thought I recognized you. That was some quick thinking, all right. Not sure why that would change anything now, though."

Dee knew exactly what she was going to say. "I'll tell you why—because if I hadn't helped you clear the road with my truck and then taken people home after the fire, I wouldn't have run out of gas on my own way home. And if I hadn't run out of gas, that man wouldn't have been able to steal the truck and bring it back here. The way I see it, you owe me, so let us in to look for it."

The big man uncrossed his arms and scratched his head. "Well, you've got a point there. I guess I might be able to let a couple of kids in for a few minutes."

"We won't be long," assured Hyrum. "Just long enough to get the truck and get out of here."

Matt squinted at the sun. "Town's got a curfew now. You have to be gone before dark or you'll spend the night locked up. We've had some trouble with break-ins and such. And you'll have to take the truck out over Old Lookout Road. This road stays blocked."

"You got it," said Hyrum at the same time Dee said, "Thanks."

Matt straightened and his voice was stern. "I'm trusting you both. And if I hear one word of you trying to take anything out of here besides the truck, I'll track you down myself and take it out of your hides."

*

The streets were empty and quiet as Dee and Hyrum coasted through the business section of town. Store windows were broken out and boarded over, and trash and litter were everywhere. "Where is everyone?" Dee felt like she should whisper.

"No idea," said Hyrum in a low voice. "I've never seen it so empty."

"It's creepy," said Dee. "Like we're being watched."

When they got to the clinic, the parking lot was full of vehicles parked randomly throughout the lot, and they saw the clinic itself was as damaged and deserted as the other businesses. Dee scanned the lot quickly, and her heart sank. Grandpa's truck was nowhere in sight.

She felt like shouting curses. "Why can't I catch a single break?"

"Let's go look inside," said Hyrum.

"How's that going to help?" asked Dee.

"Maybe we can find out where the couple lived," he replied. "They probably drove the truck back to their house after she had the baby. Come on, it can't hurt."

Inside, the clinic was a shambles compared to when Dee had last seen it. Chairs were knocked over, papers and trash strewn around. Behind the front desk, file drawers had been pulled out, contents dumped on the floor.

"This is crazy," said Dee. "We're not going to find anything here."

"Just hold on," said Hyrum. "You haven't even tried to look."

Dee snorted. "Whatever. I'm going to wait outside." But as she made her way back around the front desk, her eye fell on something half concealed by a pile of papers. She pulled a clipboard out and peered at it.

"Hyrum," she said excitedly. "I think I found something. Check it out."

It was the registration clipboard people had to fill out when they walked in. From the dates Dee could see they'd stopped taking patients over a week ago, but . . . She turned a couple pages back and found the day she wanted: June 24. Now she looked at "Reason for Visit."

They'd never put up with that in her city, with everyone paranoid about privacy, thought Dee. *Come on, come on . . .* "Here it is!" she told Hyrum excitedly. "Sally Markham Fife, reason for visit: C-section." Dee read further over and gasped. "Oh no. Oh no."

"What's wrong?" said Hyrum.

"Look," she pointed. Next to Sally's line on the chart were three letters in someone else's handwriting. "DOA," Dee said out loud. "Dead on arrival."

She leaned on the counter, tired. "It was all for nothing," she said finally. "The truck's gone and Sally and the baby are dead. What's even the point?"

Hyrum sat on the floor next to her. "Let's just talk it through," he said. "Where would you go if you were that husband?"

Dee shrugged. "I dunno."

"You told me the husband said God sent them the truck. So he's religious, right? Maybe he went somewhere to pray. There's a Catholic church not far from here."

They walked back out into the afternoon sunshine and blinked to clear their eyes after the dim interior of the clinic. Dee looked around. "You've got to be kidding me," she said flatly.

The bikes were gone.

Hyrum ran to the street and scanned both directions, but it was no use and they both knew it.

"Come on," she said, starting to walk back the way they'd come. "Forget the church. It's going to take us hours to get home as it is. Let's go."

Hyrum grabbed her arm, "Can you humor me on this? I've just got a feeling about the church. I think we're supposed to go there."

Dee looked up into Hyrum's eyes. He was serious.

"Fine," she said, shaking off his arm. "We'll go for a minute, but that's it."

It took a lot longer to cross the town on foot, and Dee found the silence of the empty streets even more oppressive. Now she was sure they were being watched.

As they approached the church, they saw three tall crosses on the grounds. A crowd was gathered near the foot of the crosses, blocking their view of what was happening. Hyrum saw someone he knew.

"The sheriff caught a thief this afternoon," Hyrum's friend said. He looked about Hyrum's age, and Dee guessed they knew each other from school. "This guy has a lot of nerve," the young man continued. "He walked right into a house and came out carrying a grocery bag of food. In broad daylight," he added in disgust.

Dee hopped up and down trying to get a glimpse of the thief. There was finally a break in the crowd and Dee got a good look at him. He stood at the base of the central cross with his hands cuffed behind the back of the cross. As Dee watched, one of the women in the crowd spat on him. Unable to wipe his face, he let the spittle drip slowly down his cheek. Dee locked eyes with him and stared in horror. Though he was thinner than he'd been a few weeks ago when they'd last seen each other, there was still no mistaking him. It was Mason.

"So how long does he have to stay here?" Hyrum was asking.

"Just for the night. Sheriff wants everyone to get a good look at the thief."

"Then what?" asked Hyrum. "Are they going to run him out of town in the morning?"

"No," Dee heard the young man next to her say. "In the morning they're going to shoot him."

CHAPTER TWELVE

"You can't be serious," Dee snapped. "That's ridiculous. You don't shoot someone for stealing food."

Another voice near Dee piped up. "That's what I've been saying. He's just a kid and he hasn't even had a trial." It was an older man in a jacket and he looked vaguely familiar.

"You're wrong, Max. We've gotta set an example. Show folks what happens to thieves."

"But public executions for minor infractions? That's taking it too far." The murmur of the crowd increased as people voiced their opinions.

Dee pushed her way to the front and stood in front of Mason. "What is going on?" she demanded.

He hissed, "What are you doing? You've got to get lost."

"For your information, I'm looking for my grandpa's truck."

Someone near her elbow asked, "Who's your grandpa?"

"Doctor Milton Kerns, the vet," she replied, turning toward the voice. There was some murmuring in the crowd and then another voice said, "Doesn't he drive an old Chevrolet? I think I saw Gerald Fife in a white truck just like it a while back."

A few more people agreed they'd seen him, too, but no one knew where he'd gone. Conversation turned to his wife, Sally, and their baby. "Poor things," one woman said. "Has anyone seen Gerald?"

"Dee," she heard Mason whisper. She glanced over her shoulder at him and he indicated with a movement of his head she should come closer. The crowd had moved on to talking about another woman who had died in childbirth. They weren't focusing on Dee for the moment. She took a backward step closer to Mason, still facing away from him, pretending to pay attention to the conversation.

Mason whispered, "The truck's in the cemetery. I left something in it for you." Dee felt her pulse quicken and she wasn't sure whether it was his closeness or discovering where the truck was. "West side of town. Take it and get out of here," he said roughly.

She felt a surge of anger. She wanted to ask him why he'd left on the day of the EMP and why he'd been stealing food. Where were his parents? Shouldn't they be dealing with this?

There were too many people listening, though, and she had to go. She felt guilty about leaving, but the last time she'd left Grandpa alone this long he'd had a heart attack. Besides, Mason had left her first. She wasn't going to risk getting involved with him again.

Dee told herself that the older man, Max, and some of the others would be able to get the crowd to come to its senses. She turned and worked her way back to Hyrum.

"He told me where the truck is," she whispered to Hyrum.

"Do you know Mason?" he asked, eyebrows raised.

"Barely. We only met once." She tried to sound nonchalant and hoped the flush she could feel in her cheeks wouldn't give her away. "Never mind that," she said impatiently. "Let's go see if the truck's still there."

*

It took them about ten minutes to walk the five blocks to the cemetery, all of it seemingly uphill. When they got there, Dee was surprised to see that the cemetery covered a large area, full of hills and trees. It took another ten minutes before they found the truck in a back corner under a large weeping willow. Its branches hid the truck almost entirely. Just the lower halves of its tires were showing. If she hadn't known where to look she doubted she would have noticed it.

She went immediately to the bed of the truck and inspected the lockbox. It didn't seem damaged. After looking around to make sure they were alone, she set the key in the lock and turned. The food was still there.

"What's in there?" asked Hyrum.

"Just some supplies," she said. Dee trusted Hyrum, but she was learning that hunger changed people. She locked the storage box again and went back around to the driver side, where Hyrum was trying to get the door open.

"See right here?" he pointed. "Someone used a slim jim to unlock the door, but I don't see it anywhere."

"Grandpa only had the one set of keys," Dee sighed. This was the biggest flaw with her plan. She'd been hoping the car thief had left the keys in the truck. If they weren't there, they'd have to bring the food back one load at a time. And now, without the bikes, it would be a huge job.

"I'm going to bust the window and see if the key's inside," said Hyrum, looking for a rock.

"Hold on," said Dee. "Do you smell something?" A gust of wind brought a foul stench to them and Dee looked around for the source.

"Down there," pointed Hyrum. "But I'm not sure we want to get any closer."

Dee was already moving downhill toward the still form.

It was a sad scene, needing no explanation. Next to a grave with a fresh mound of dirt and a bouquet of wilted wildflowers was the body of the man who had stolen the truck. He was lying stretched out beside the grave, and the back of his head was blown out.

Dee cupped a hand over her nose and mouth and felt tears sting her eyes, either from the tragedy or the smell, or maybe both. She wondered how many women with no access to medical care had died in childbirth in the past several weeks. How many people had taken their own lives in despair? How many good people had stolen food or supplies, leaving others to starve?

"I don't see the gun," said Hyrum practically, inspecting the scene. "Come on, we've got to figure out how to get that truck out of here."

"I think I've got an idea," Dee said, looking at the pitiful figure on the ground. She pulled the collar of her shirt up over her nose and walked closer to the man. He was lying on his side, facing the mound of dirt, and had one arm protectively wrapped over it. Dee looked at the other hand, and though it was near his head, Hyrum was right—there was no sign of a gun. She didn't care about the gun, though. Trying not to gag, she leaned over the decomposing corpse and reached into its pants pocket. *Please don't make me roll it over,* she thought. She felt something thin and metallic and pulled it out. The key!

She and Hyrum ran back to the truck. The key worked perfectly and they climbed inside. Propped on the dashboard in front of the speedometer was an envelope addressed to Dee.

"He can't be serious," she said under her breath. More than anything she wanted to start the truck and get out of there, but she couldn't leave Mason to die without at least reading the note. "Give me a second, okay?" she told Hyrum. Then she read:

Dear Dee, I wish I could explain everything to you, but there's too much to say and no time. I know I can trust you to do one favor for me. Under the seat is a pack of food. Please take it to the house at 311 Elm and give it to the woman there. Her name is Jess. She's my mom.

Dee set the note down carefully and sat, unseeing. Why hadn't he told her about his mom?

"Is there a pack of food under the seat?" she asked Hyrum.

He felt around and pulled it out. "Yep."

"We've got to do something before we go."

Hyrum sighed. "I was afraid you were going to say that."

*

311 Elm was a run-down house in what was obviously the poor part of town. A sagging chain-link fence surrounded the house, and a rusted tricycle sat alone on the hard-packed dirt driveway. Broken chairs, empty boxes, and a rotting couch littered the front yard. The roof showed signs of water damage, and an old satellite TV dish drooped sadly over the cracked plastic rain gutter.

Hyrum and Dee stood in the road staring at the house. It was only a few blocks from the cemetery, so they'd walked over rather than risk having the truck stolen. They'd learned that lesson the hard way.

"Are you sure about this, Dee?"

"Not really," she said, squaring her shoulders and taking a deep breath. There'd obviously been no trash removal for weeks and the smell of overflowing garbage cans up and down the block was overpowering.

As she approached the house she came around the side of one of the cardboard boxes and jumped back, startled. There was a little boy sitting inside with thin legs drawn up under his chin and something crumpled in his hand. He wasn't crying, but Dee could see the tracks of tears on his grubby cheeks.

She glanced at the empty doorway of the house and then squatted down next to the boy. "Hey there," she said. "Whatcha doing in here?"

"This used to belong to my dog," he said, handing her a dirty dog collar with "Indy" engraved on it. "I think bad guys got him," he said, with a loud sniff.

"Bad guys?" said Dee.

"They come at night lookin' for food, but my dad and his friends already made off with most all of it. Me and Mom and Indy hide under the stairs 'til they go."

"Your dad took your food?" Dee was horrified. "All of it?"

The boy nodded.

"Is your mom inside?"

"Yeah, but she's sick. She told me to go outside and watch for Mason."

"You know Mason?"

"'Course I do," the little boy said, puffing out his thin chest. "He's my big brother."

"Does he live here with you?" asked Dee, looking at the broken house.

"He's not allowed. My dad said he'll beat Mama if Mason comes 'round anymore." He lowered his voice and whispered, "Mason still comes, though. He sneaks in at night and leaves us food. Mama said he stole it back from Hank."

"Hank?" asked Dee.

"My dad," said the child. "He's Mason's stepdad. He's living with a lady over on the other side of town, but he still comes by to see if we've got somethin' to eat." He shrugged a thin shoulder. "Ain't nothin' left now anyway."

Dee studied the child and guessed he was five, maybe six years old. It was hard to tell since he was so small. She looked into the bag of food Mason had left for his family and pulled out an energy bar. "Mason sent me to talk to your mama. Can you stay out here and eat this while I go talk to her?"

The boy sat very still, eyeing the food. "Are you trickin'?" he said finally.

Dee handed the bar to the little boy and blinked rapidly to clear her sudden tears. "I'm not trickin'. My friend is going to stay here with you, okay?"

The child peered out from the box at Hyrum and gave a nod. "He looks okay." Then he unwrapped the bar and began wolfing it down.

"I'll be right back," Dee told Hyrum, and climbed the rickety wooden steps to the broken screen door. There was no answer to her knock, so she called and went inside, stepping over toys and litter in the front room. The kitchen was filled with stinking dishes, empty cans, and old wrappers, but a worse smell was coming from the hallway. Dee walked slowly toward the bedrooms, dreading what she'd find.

Dee found Mason's mom in bed, lying in her own filth. She'd obviously been sick, and the stench of vomit and diarrhea was almost too much for Dee, but it was the sight of the woman's bruised face and dead, unseeing eyes that made her flee the room. She left at a run, barely making it to the kitchen to vomit in the sink. She looked for something to rinse her mouth and saw a bucket of dirty water on the counter, along with some drinking glasses. Had they been drinking this sludge?

Outside, Hyrum and the boy were kicking an old soccer ball around the yard. When he saw her, Hyrum raised his brows in a question and Dee shook her head slightly. He bent and picked up the soccer ball and then squatted down next to the boy. "Hey, little man, wanna go with us? We're going to find your brother."

CHAPTER THIRTEEN

Dee was relieved she didn't have to try to talk Hyrum into a rescue mission. He'd been listening when Sammy explained that Mason had only taken back the food his stepdad had stolen from his own wife and family. Mason was innocent and now that the boys' mother was dead, Mason was Sammy's only family. There wasn't a chance that they'd sit back and let Mason get shot in the morning.

Back at the cemetery, they put Sammy in the cab of the truck, where he polished off a bottle of water and then a snack-sized can of cold ravioli before curling up for a nap on the seat. Dee and Hyrum sat on the truck's tailgate and shared what they knew about Mason. It didn't amount to much. Hyrum said he'd seen Mason around school a few times, but he'd dropped out in the middle of the year. Some folks said he was being homeschooled, but he hadn't made a lot of friends and no one was interested enough to see if he was okay.

Hyrum balled one hand into a fist and punched it into the palm of his other hand in frustration. "Did you know my mom's a teacher? If she saw someone playing alone at recess, guess who she called to go play with him?" He pointed at his own chest and nodded. "I made a lot of friends that way, just being a friend. After Dad died though, I just . . . I dunno. It was harder. I needed some space. I saw Mason around now and then, and I had a feeling he could use a friend but I ignored it."

Dee put a hand on his forearm and felt the tension there. "You know none of this is your fault, right? You can't blame yourself. Obviously, this Hank guy has issues. How could you have known?"

"At least Mason would have had a friend after his stepdad kicked him out. He could have stayed with us instead of living in the woods."

"Listen," said Dee. "We're going to get him out of there, and then you can make it up to him."

"Any idea how we're supposed to do that?"

"Are you kidding? I don't have the first clue."

They were quiet for a few minutes and then Hyrum said, "Remember in *The Princess Bride* when Inigo, Fezzik, and Westley are planning to rescue Buttercup?"

Dee rolled her eyes. "Seriously? Are you really going to compare this to an '80s movie?"

"No, but it made me think of something. Remember how Westley wants to know what their assets are? I think that's where we need to start—what are our assets?"

Dee quipped, "My brains, your strength?"

Hyrum punched her lightly in the arm. "Ha-ha, very funny. Be serious. What have we got?" Hyrum started numbering things on his fingers. "First, we have a getaway car. Second, we've got a backpack of food. Third . . ."

Dee interrupted, pointing at the farm tools in the truck bed. "Look at all this stuff back here. We could use those wrenches as clubs, and there's some more food in the storage box."

"Any alcohol or beer?" asked Hyrum.

Dee shook her head.

"Dang it, that always works in movies."

"Guess you'll just have to use your charm," Dee said.

*

The back of the truck yielded one real prize—a pair of bolt cutters. Dee and Hyrum spent the rest of the evening in the cemetery, talking over plans and contingencies. In the end they decided to go with something simple. Hyrum would draw the guard off and then outrun him, while Dee sneaked in with the bolt cutters and set Mason free. They'd meet back at the truck and go from there.

They stayed in the cemetery until after sunset, both too on-edge to take a nap, though they were facing a long night. Dee hoped that her grandpa wasn't too worried about her. She knew stress was bad for his heart. At least Jeremiah was there to do the evening chores.

Once it was dark enough, Dee put the truck in neutral and quietly let it roll downhill through the streets, careful to avoid vehicles that had been abandoned in the road. Each time the truck creaked or groaned she knew they were going to be caught and locked up for being out after curfew. The road stayed quiet, though, and there was no sign anyone had seen or heard them.

They stopped the truck next to a curb just around the corner from the church.

"I hope he's still there," Hyrum muttered.

"Who's there?" asked Sammy. He'd awakened after a long and much-needed nap and rubbed at his eyes.

"Can you keep a secret, Sammy?" Dee asked. "Hyrum and I are going to go get a surprise for you, but only if you stay here in the truck and be extra quiet."

Sammy practically bounced with excitement and Dee wondered if she'd used the wrong approach.

"Is the surprise candy?" he asked.

"No, it's—"

"Is it a toy?"

"No—"

"Is it a—"

"Sammy," Dee interrupted in a firm tone. "I'm not going to tell you or it won't be a surprise. But it might take us a while, and you have to promise to stay right here in the truck, okay?"

"Okay." Sammy nodded. He sat still on the seat but his little body was tense and sometimes his legs kicked out excitedly.

Hyrum shook his head. "Now he's all worked up."

"He'll stay here. Won't you, Sammy?" Dee said, eyeing the little boy doubtfully.

"I won't move a stitch." Sammy crossed his arms over his chest and froze in place.

"All right, all right," said Hyrum, smothering a laugh. When he glanced at Dee she saw that despite his laugh, his eyes were sad. She thought about Sammy's mom and felt her own heart grow heavy.

Hyrum and Dee watched the church from their vantage point, hidden in the shadows of a fence across the street. The grounds were still and eerie, bathed in silver light from the nearly full moon. The church itself was less mystical—a blocky, beige building hunkered down next to a large parking lot. On one side of the covered entrance to the church was a circular area landscaped with trampled marigolds, gravel, and three crosses in a row, stretching up at least twenty feet high.

Dee thought the attempt at religious decoration rather unfortunate. The crosses were tilted and obviously old, with peeling white paint that was chipped in places. Mason was still there, and he looked as thin and tired as the crosses. Dee wanted to tell him to hold on, they were coming for him.

Two guards sat near the entrance of the building on folding chairs with a small table between them, engrossed in a game of cards in the light of a small lantern. Hyrum held out his hand, motioning for Dee to hand him the bolt cutters. He whispered that he thought the guards were distracted already, and he would try to set Mason free on his own. If they spotted him, he'd drop the bolt cutters and run, drawing them away from their post.

Dee's heart skipped in her chest. They were really going to do this. She watched as Hyrum slipped across the street and through the parking lot. Abandoned cars provided some cover, but in the bright moonlight Hyrum was more exposed than not. Mason suddenly stood up straight and Dee knew he'd spotted Hyrum's approach. He was about thirty feet away from the crosses and easing his way carefully through the last section of the parking lot.

Just then, Hyrum brought his shoe down on a piece of broken glass. The crunching sound was loud in the darkness, and the guards looked up from their cards. They saw Hyrum instantly. The first one jumped to his feet and headed for Hyrum while the second spoke into his radio. Hyrum waited, and though Dee willed him to run, she knew he had to lure both guards away. When the first guard was almost close enough to touch, Hyrum sprinted straight toward him and veered, heading for the second guard.

He's trying to make them mad, thought Dee when he tipped over the card table before jogging across the church grounds. The guards were slow on their feet and Dee guessed they hadn't been eating as well as Hyrum. Nor were they running for their lives.

When Hyrum knocked over the table, Dee made her way quickly across the street and into the parking lot. She didn't know how long he'd be able to keep the guards busy; she had to be fast. The bolt cutters were on the ground where Hyrum had dropped them. Dee picked them up and covered the short distance to Mason.

"What's wrong with you?" he hissed. "Get out of here, they'll be back any minute."

Dee ignored him. She had a bigger problem—the bolt cutters wouldn't open.

"Are you kidding?" she groaned as she tried to pull the handles apart.

"What's wrong?" Mason said, trying to peer over his shoulder at her.

"It's these . . . stupid . . ."

"Are you sure the latch is off?"

Dee held the tool out of her shadow and saw the plastic latch. She slid it open and tried again, but the cutters still wouldn't budge.

"It's off," Dee grunted. "I think they're rusted or something."

"Never mind," Mason said, scanning the area anxiously. "Leave 'em and get out of here. I'll be fine."

Dee braced one of the handles under her tennis shoe and gave short, fierce pulls on the other handle. "Not . . . going to . . ." she said, struggling. ". . . leave you," she finished in triumph as the bolt cutters snapped open. She positioned the blades around the chain that secured Mason to the cross. It looked like it came from a child's swing set.

"Hold still," she barked at Mason, who was trying to keep his wrists out of the way of the blades. It was awkward, and she didn't think she had enough hand strength to cut the chain.

"I've got an idea—just hang on," said Dee. She put one handle of the tool against the cross between Mason's hands, and put her foot up on the other handle. "Come . . . on!" She pushed with all her strength. The bolt cutter snapped shut and the chain fell to the ground.

"Let's go!" She grabbed Mason's hand to lead him away but he was frozen in place.

Dee looked up and saw three men with guns trained on them.

She raised her hands but wasn't ready to give up. "You have the wrong guy. Mason didn't steal that food."

"That's not what we heard, little lady," drawled one of the men. He was lean, well-muscled and wore tight Wranglers and a belt with a huge buckle. It didn't look like he'd missed any meals lately.

Mason was shushing her and shaking his head, but Dee wasn't finished.

"His stepdad stole it from him and he was just taking it back."

"Is that right, now?" A man with a plaid shirt and cowboy hat chuckled. "That's not what his stepdad says."

"Come on, guys. Let her go. She doesn't know anything. I took the food—you got me. Just let her go."

"'Fraid not," said the man with the belt buckle. He pulled out some rope and tied Dee and Mason to two of the crosses. "We're just gonna wait here for the sheriff."

"I thought he wasn't coming back 'til morning," said Mason.

The man lit a cigarette and took a drag. "Said he didn't want to miss the fun."

A few minutes later they heard a car engine approaching and then a cop car pulled up in front of the church. Dee went over what she was going to say to him. Once he heard how Mason's stepdad had mistreated his family, he'd at least have to give Mason the benefit of the doubt and a stay of execution.

A bulky form in an officer's uniform got out of the car and pulled someone out of the backseat. Dee's heart sank. It was Hyrum. How had they caught him? Their rescue attempt was a big, fat failure. The officer led Hyrum to the crosses and gave orders for him to be tied up, as well. Then he faced the three captives. Dee could see the word *SHERIFF* stitched on his uniform and knew it was now or never. She opened her mouth to make her case for Mason's release, just as Mason spoke.

"Nice of you to stop by, Hank."

CHAPTER FOURTEEN

Dee's mind reeled as she tried to make sense of it all. Mason's stepdad, Hank, was the sheriff?

They were in serious trouble.

"I didn't know you had a girlfriend, boy. She any good?" Hank moved to stand in front of Dee and caress her cheek.

At Hank's taunt, Mason strained against his bonds. "You leave her out of this," he shouted. "This is between you and me."

Dee yanked her face away from Hank and stomped on his foot.

Hank leaned closer, his foul breath hot on her face. "Your girlfriend tried to hurt me, Mason. You should tell her how much I enjoy a challenge." Then, before she knew what was happening, he slapped her hard across the cheek.

It took a moment for Dee's head to clear, and when it did she was furious. No one had ever hit her before. Her cheek stung like crazy and it felt like her heart was beating in her face. She glared at Hank so intently she didn't even see the next blow coming. This one was harder, and snapped her head to the side.

"She has spirit, I'll give you that," Hank said to Mason before turning to Hyrum. "Who's your other friend here?" He felt Hyrum's biceps. "Unless I miss my guess, you've got some food put away somewhere."

Hyrum tensed at the touch but said in an even tone, "I can get food for you, too, if you let us all go."

"Oh, you'll get food for me, all right. After that I might let you go. Just you—not Mason. And not the girl. Mason and I have an appointment in a few hours I know he's looking forward to." He held his hand up like a pistol and pointed it at Mason. "Bam." Then he turned back to Dee. "As for this tasty morsel, I've got something in mind for her, too. Something real nice."

Dee shuddered at the sick innuendo in his tone and Hyrum said quickly, "Her for me. Let her go and keep me. I'm a hard worker; I'll run your errands and track down food and water for you. Guns, too," he added quickly.

"How do I know you'll stick around?" said Hank.

"You have my word," said Hyrum, standing up straight.

"I'll think it over," said Hank, looking Hyrum up and down. "I can always use a good man. Of course," he continued, "by then I'll be done with the girl anyway." His twisted laughter rang out across the parking lot.

He turned back to Mason. "You wanna tell her what she has to look forward to? What I done to your ma?"

Mason's voice was cold and hard. "If you touch her, I swear I'll kill you."

"And how do you think you're gonna do that, eh? You'll be dead in a few hours, just like your mom." Dee looked horrified at Mason. The color drained from his face and his legs bent like he might collapse. "You're lying," he said in a weak voice.

"You know I'm not, boy. Look at my face. Tell me, am I lying?" His eyes glittered. "That's right, your mom's dead, and so's your little bastard brother."

Mason made a sound that started low in his throat and ripped out of him like a howl. It was pure pain.

Dee tried to think clearly. Could Hank have found Sammy or was he lying to mess with Mason? She fought to keep from turning to look toward the truck. Wasn't it parked out of sight around the corner and down the street?

Dee prayed.

Please, God, let that little boy be safe. No matter what happens to us, please look out for him.

Just then, the man with the belt buckle walked up to Hank and said something quietly in his ear. "You sure, Mitchell?" said Hank.

The man nodded. "Call just came in over the CB."

Hank turned toward the three teenagers. "I want you to think about what we discussed. I've gotta go for a while, but I'll be back soon and we can pick up where we left off." He gave Dee a meaningful look. "I'll be looking forward to it."

He jerked his head at the man in the plaid shirt and two other men. "Let's go. Mitchell can stay here and keep an eye on things, right?"

Mitchell nodded. "No problem, boss."

"See you kids in a few hours," said Hank, and then he was gone.

*

Dee slid down the base of the cross until she was sitting cross-legged on the ground. She didn't think her legs could hold her any more. She was tired and angry and confused, and she just wanted to leave.

Mason had his head turned away from them and his shoulders shook. Dee wanted to tell him his brother was fine, but she didn't know for sure. If Hank had found the truck, wouldn't he have mentioned it? But, thought Dee, Hank wasn't sane. There was no telling what he'd do.

Hyrum worked his way around his cross until he was facing them and glanced over at the guard. "We've got to get out of here," he said in a low voice.

"No kidding," said Dee. "Got any suggestions?"

"Can you feel any sharp rocks or anything you could use to cut through the rope?" he asked.

Dee felt around, but the gravel she was sitting in was made of tiny, smooth pebbles. "Nothing here," she said.

"I'm going to see if I can lean on my cross and push it over." Dee saw Hyrum's muscles strain and his face turn red, but the cross didn't move. It was old, but solid.

"It's no use," he said, panting softly and sliding down to sit on the ground like Dee.

"There's no point," Mason said, his voice flat. "Hank is pure evil. Learn from my mistakes. Just give him what he wants and then get as far from him as you can. You can't beat him."

"You're wrong, Mason," said Hyrum with conviction. "We *can* beat him. You've just got to have faith."

"Yeah, right," said Mason bitterly. "Is faith going to stop a bullet to my brain in a few hours? Is faith going to feed the starving people in this town being terrorized by my stepdad?" His voice was rising. "Is faith going to bring back my mom and brother?"

"Shut your traps over there," said Mitchell. He had the CB up to his ear and was listening intently.

"Do you guys want to say a prayer with me?" asked Hyrum. Mason snorted and turned his head away but Dee kept her eyes fixed on Hyrum. He sounded so calm and sure and she wanted to believe. She wanted to believe they could get away from here. She wanted to believe Sammy was alive. She wanted to believe she'd see her parents again.

Hyrum bowed his head and prayed so softly Dee could barely catch the words. His eyes were closed so he didn't see when Mitchell stood up and approached, CB in hand. "I'm stepping away for five minutes so don't go nowhere," he said with a smirk. Then he turned and walked quickly away across the parking lot.

"And now we're supposed to believe he left because of your prayer, right?" Mason's tone was bitter and hard. He didn't seem anything like the guy Dee had picked up in the truck a few weeks ago. "Lucky coincidence, that's all. And a coincidence isn't going to cut these ropes off."

"Believe what you want," said Hyrum, and Dee noticed he was watching something beyond Mason and starting to smile.

Dee followed Hyrum's gaze and couldn't believe her eyes. It was Sammy hurrying toward them from around the side of the church. He was approaching from behind Mason, so he didn't see him right away.

"Is it almost time for the surprise?" Sammy asked.

Mason gasped at the sound of Sammy's voice and tried to get a glimpse of him.

Hyrum grinned. "It sure is. Look who we found."

Sammy spotted Mason and gave a squeal before hugging him, his face practically split in two with the biggest smile Dee had ever seen.

CHAPTER FIFTEEN

Once Sammy figured out where Hank had kicked the bolt cutters, Mason was able to pry them open again. (Dee figured she must have loosened them up a little.) Then he used the blade to saw awkwardly at the rope binding his hands until it parted and he was free. It was short work to cut Hyrum and Dee free, and they all made it safely to the truck.

Mason looked at Sammy constantly, as though trying to memorize everything about him. In the truck, he held his little brother on his lap while Hyrum drove them all back to the farm, staying on side roads as much as possible. At one point Mason said quietly to Dee, "If Hank lied about Sammy, maybe he was lying about . . ." Dee interrupted him with a hand on his arm and a shake of her head.

"I'm so sorry, Mason," she said in a subdued tone.

Mason held Sammy more tightly and stared out the window into the darkness the rest of the way to the farm.

*

Late the next morning the two families met at Grandpa's house to discuss the events of the previous day and the two new additions to their households. It was decided that since Grandpa's house had three empty bedrooms and the Searles were doubled up at theirs, Mason and Sammy would stay with the Kernses.

Sammy was delighted. He and Jasper had discovered each other immediately, and the child was already asking Grandpa if Jasper knew how to round up chickens.

"I want you two boys to get some rest today and tomorrow before you start work," Grandpa said, after he'd had a good look at Mason and his brother. "You're nothing but skin and bones, and I don't want to lose two good farm hands to a strong gust of wind."

Sammy looked down at his hands with concern and then stuffed them in his pockets. "My farm hands will be safe in here."

Grandpa let loose the loudest laugh Dee had heard from him since his heart attack. She could already see it would be good for him to have the little boy around. Last night, she'd considered telling him that Hank and his men might come after them. One look told her that their late night had put a strain on him, and she didn't want him to worry about something that might never happen. The farm was a long way from town, and she didn't think Hank knew who she was or where she was staying.

As for Mason, he prowled the farmhouse restlessly until Dee offered him a tour. She tried talking to him while she showed him around, but his responses were clipped and negative. While she didn't blame him for being withdrawn, she remembered what he'd been like with her on the day of the EMP. Her heart ached for his losses and she wondered how to help him.

He'd been really handy fixing the truck after the wreck, she remembered. Seeds of an idea formed in her mind.

"Are we about done here?" Mason asked. "Not much of a farm, is it?"

Dee tried to keep her tone polite. "Almost. There's just one more thing I wanted to show you."

Mason looked to see where they were heading. "You mean that old shack? What is it? A retired train car? I'm pretty sure if you've seen one run-down farm shed, you've seen them all."

"Have you got somewhere better to be?" Dee instantly regretted her sharp tone. Mason shrugged and looked away.

They were almost to the shed now and Dee crossed her fingers. When Mason opened the door he gave a low whistle of appreciation and Dee grinned. While she'd originally dismissed the tool shed and its rusty, outdated contents, Mason was like a kid in a candy store. He opened the door and shutters wide to let in the light and spent the afternoon poking around farm implements and then looking over old machinery left to rust in the fields.

It seemed to help his mood, because at dinner that night Mason wolfed down scrambled eggs and outlined some of his ideas for improving farm processes. He felt certain he could get an old chainsaw working, as well as a small rototiller for the garden. "That's not even the best part," he said around a mouthful of food. "I think I saw something out there I can use to get the well working again."

"Wait, say that again," said Dee. She'd been distracted by Sammy and Jasper. Despite having been close to starvation, the little boy couldn't resist slipping occasional bites of egg to the dog, whose head rested politely, but insistently, on Sammy's leg.

"I think I found an old pump handle," said Mason. "It was jumbled together with a bunch of piping and other scrap metal."

"I'd forgotten all about that old pump handle," said Grandpa, setting his fork down abruptly. "We updated the well . . . Why, it must have been at least thirty years ago. It was a big day for us, putting in an electric pump."

"So that handle used to fit the current well?" Mason asked. "If so, there's a real good chance I can rig it up manually."

"Hold on," said Dee. "Are you saying we might be able to get clean water out of the well? No more hauling it from the ditch and boiling it? No more water that tastes like dirt?"

Mason nodded. "We'll still have to haul it in, but at least it won't be straight out of the creek anymore."

Dee was so happy she felt like getting up and doing a dance. She settled for giving Mason a bright smile and a high five.

"Now I know how people felt when the dishwasher was invented," she said.

*

While Mason investigated the farm, Dee spent the morning bringing food and supplies in from the truck. She'd bought everything in such a hurry and it had been so long ago that she had no idea what to expect. As she piled everything on the kitchen counter, some of the supplies baffled her, but others made her want to sing out loud.

When she had all the groceries inside, the first thing she did was make a pot of coffee. It was just instant coffee and boiled creek water, but she made it strong and used plenty of fresh cream and sugar. Dee wrapped her hands around the warm mug and lifted it up to her face until she could feel the heat rising from it. She inhaled deeply. Pure heaven.

It had been weeks since she'd had her last cup of coffee, and she reflected on how much had changed since then. She'd gone from being a city girl scared of gas stoves and cows to a farmer and survivor.

Dee liked this side of herself. She felt strong, and she wished her parents could see her. What would they think of her now?

A few minutes later Grandpa found her in the kitchen, cup in hand, staring at the supplies on the counter. He made himself a cup of coffee and sat next to her. "What's going on in that head of yours?" he asked.

"I was remembering the day I bought all this. It seemed like so much. I felt like I was buying enough to feed a family for a whole year, but now I'm looking at it and it doesn't seem like much at all. Without the animals and garden this wouldn't last more than a month or two." She looked at him and spoke more quickly. "Especially with Mason and Sammy. Thank you so much for taking them in. If you'd seen Sammy sitting in the box that day while his mom was . . . the way she was . . . And without Mason we wouldn't have this food or the truck or anything. And his dad is totally messed up. I had to bring them."

Grandpa put his warm, wrinkled hand over Dee's. "You did exactly right, Maddie-girl. Your folks would be real proud to see the kind of woman you're turnin' into. Almost as proud as I am."

Dee hid her face in her cup so Grandpa wouldn't see her tears.

*

Angela Searle answered her front door with a warm smile. "Hi, Maddie, what a nice surprise. Come on in."

It was Dee's first time inside the Searle home and she looked around with interest. The main living area had comfortable-looking chairs and a couch, and the walls were decorated with photos of the family. Hyrum and his brothers looked a lot like their dad. There was another son Dee hadn't met, and she knew he must be the one in California. Dee noted decorative cross-stitches with messages such as "Love One Another" and "Families Are Forever." What most caught her eye was a large painting of Jesus over the fireplace. In it, Christ held a small oil lamp aloft while offering her his other hand. He seemed to be looking right at her, with a faint but kindly smile. She was mesmerized.

"Do you like it?" Angela was asking.

"It's . . . different," Dee said finally. "He looks so nice."

"I love the way this artist portrays Christ. Like a loving older brother instead of an angry God or a victim being tortured on the cross."

Dee shifted her weight, and Angela changed the subject. "Well, I'm sure you aren't here to talk religion. Hang on a sec and I'll call Hyrum."

"Actually," Dee interjected, "I came to talk to you about something."

"Oh?" said Angela, eyebrows raised.

"Do you remember when you agreed to teach me to cook?" said Dee awkwardly. "I'm pretty awful at it, but we're all getting a little tired of eating eggs for every meal."

Angela laughed. "I thought you'd never ask. No worries, it's not that hard once you get the hang of it."

"Famous last words," said Dee.

"Give yourself some credit. I bet you'll be surprised," said Angela with a smile. "I believe half of what makes a good cook is being able to identify good recipes. Once you've got the right recipe it's just a matter of following directions. If you want, we can start today."

For the first lesson, Dee didn't do any cooking at all. She and Angela sat down with a pen and paper and made a list of the staples Dee had access to, including the food in the garden. Then they went through Angela's cookbooks and Dee picked out a few recipes she wanted to try. She could hardly wait to get started when she realized she had everything she needed to make spaghetti, chili, and even chicken enchiladas.

Angela interrupted Dee's food dreams. "Before you start, there are a couple of things I want you to keep in mind. This summer and fall while there's plenty of fresh food available I recommend that you stick to eating out of the garden. Keep eating eggs, even if you're tired of them. You'll thank me this winter when the chickens stop laying and the cow dries up, but you still have food in your pantry.

"Second, stick to easy recipes. Food is too precious to waste on complicated dishes that might not turn out. Find out what your household will eat and don't aim for anything fancy."

Dee found a recipe for a rice dish with a lot of fresh vegetables in it and thought it would go well with a side of grilled zucchini and tomatoes.

"Good choices," Angela said, nodding. "Get the ingredients together, and I'll come by tomorrow afternoon. I think it's important you practice cooking at your house with your own equipment. That'll help you figure out what you can do and what won't work."

At the end of the lesson Angela flipped through a three-ring binder until she found a couple pages about solar ovens. "I'm glad I printed these out when I had the chance. Our computer hasn't worked since June."

"At least you had one," said Dee. "Grandpa didn't even have a working radio until we brought the truck back."

"Have you picked up any stations?"

"Not yet, but Mason's working on a new antenna to increase our range."

"I get the impression he's pretty handy," said Angela.

Dee nodded and Angela handed her some sheets of paper.

"Give him these instructions and tell him to help you make your own solar oven. We can use it to cook some rice tomorrow. And then later if you want, we can experiment with making cheese. With a little practice, maybe you can bake a pizza in your oven soon."

Dee hugged Angela right on the spot.

*

The next morning, Mason reviewed the list of materials needed for the solar oven. He'd started to brighten up a little and Dee was looking forward to working on a project with him.

"Let's see here," he said. "Did you see a working version of this at the Searles'? It sounds like you basically just get a box, line the inside with black paper to absorb heat, and cover the flaps with aluminum foil to reflect the sunlight down into the box. The only tricky thing will be finding the right-size piece of glass or clear plastic to cover the opening and trap the heat inside."

"I'm sure we can scavenge most of this stuff from the house and the barn," said Dee.

"Let me think for a minute," Mason said. Dee watched while he rubbed his chin and appeared lost in thought. She wondered if he had any idea how cute he was when he did that.

"Hey," he said abruptly, "do you mind if we try doing this a little different? I think I saw something in the truck that might make it easier."

"Sure." Dee shrugged. "Why not?"

"Give me just a minute," he said and then went out to find supplies. When he came back he had a clear plastic bag, a metal grill from a small barbecue, some safety pins and a silver windshield reflector from Grandpa's truck.

"Is that going to work?" asked Dee.

"Guess we'll find out." Mason grinned and got to work. Dee was happy to see him smile. He'd been through a lot, but life on the farm seemed to suit him. He'd gained back a little weight, and he teased Sammy like an older brother should. He still needed a shave and a haircut, but now he looked rugged rather than bedraggled.

She watched as he took the reflector and pinned the short ends together so it was vaguely funnel-shaped, with the reflective side facing in. She waited to see what else he would do, but he just handed her the funnel and brushed his hands off.

"That's it. If I'm right, this thing will reflect heat just as well as the fancier deal, and it's more portable. Come on, let's go try it."

Mason put some rocks in a circle and set the reflector carefully on top, part of it bent flat. Then he put the metal grill over the flat place on the bottom of the reflector, so it rested on the rocks and made a solid place for a pot or pan. After he cracked two eggs into a cast iron pan, he wrapped it in a clear plastic bag and set it on the grill. "Here goes nothing."

Dee sat on the ground next to the grill and put a hand near the plastic. "You're better than MacGyver," she said.

"I used to love watching reruns of that show," Mason said, smiling. "When I was little I'd play MacGyver in my backyard while my mom was at work." He picked up some twigs and used them to build the walls of a mini log cabin. Not meeting her eyes, he asked, "So did you see her? My mom?"

Dee nodded, her throat tight.

"Do you think she suffered?"

They were all suffering, weren't they? Dee thought about her own mom and wondered if she was alive, or if someday she'd have a conversation like this with someone who'd seen her body. "I don't know," she said finally. "I saw a bucket of river water in the kitchen and I think maybe she'd been drinking it. She was in bed, so I think she was sick. She didn't look hurt or anything."

Dee didn't mention the vomit and filth in the bed or on the floor. She didn't mention how bruised his mom's face was or how she'd found Sammy too scared to go into his own house.

"I'm going to kill that son of a—" Mason swore. "It's his fault she's dead. The day of the EMP I went down to the sporting goods store and picked up MREs and a couple of bottles of water purifying tablets. I also grabbed a load of canned soup and vegetables from the dollar store. It wasn't gourmet, but we had enough for a while."

Mason hunched his shoulders. "I tried to convince her to get out of town with me. I know a lot of good places to camp around here where no one would have found us. We could've caught fish and lived off the land until winter. Then we could have holed up someplace safe with our survival food."

"Why wouldn't she go?" asked Dee.

"She was scared."

"Of Hank?"

Mason shook his head with a hint of a smile. "Actually, bears and moose. She hated camping. She would have been miserable."

"So she stayed in town with Sammy?"

"Yeah, and I couldn't stay with them because Hank told me he'd hurt them if he caught me at the house. I found your grandpa's truck down in the cemetery and rolled it back under the trees. It was a dry, safe place to sleep and pretty close to the house so I could keep an eye on them. I hid the supplies at the house, but somehow Hank must've found them and cleaned them out. They had next to nothing for a few days. When I found out what he'd done, I totally lost it. I didn't make a plan or anything. I just went to his girlfriend's house and broke down the door. And guess what I saw inside? You won't believe it, Dee."

"What?"

"All the food. It was like a mini-mart in there. No one was around so I filled my pack as fast as I could and got out of there. I stashed the bag in the truck and decided to go back and get everything he'd taken from us. I couldn't let him get away with it. That's when I wrote you the note, in case something happened. I knew it was a long shot, but I hoped you'd find the truck."

Mason was on his feet by now, pacing. "He was waiting for me when I went back."

"Why didn't he just put you in jail? That thing at the church was weird."

"I know, right?" said Mason. "I'm sure part of it was to humiliate me. But now I think he had a more practical reason. Think about it: Which building in town is probably the most secure?"

"The jail?" said Dee, not understanding.

"Exactly. I think after I broke in he decided to move the supplies somewhere safer. The jail would be the perfect place, but with the supplies there he can't use it to lock people up."

"What I don't get is why the town doesn't get rid of him," said Dee. "Why keep a thief around as sheriff?"

"That's the tricky part," said Mason. "They have no idea what he's doing. He's the ringleader, and he's keeping it secret. People invite him over to check out a complaint and he scopes their supplies. A few nights later he sends in his guys to rob them. No one makes the connection."

Dee shook her head. "That's just so wrong. You need to tell people what he's doing."

"And then what? Look at me. I'm a runaway, a nobody. They're not going to take my word over the sheriff's. Plus, you saw what he's capable of, Dee. We need to stay as far away from him as possible." Mason said in a low voice, "Sometimes I have nightmares that he shows up here at the farm. He has vehicles, Dee. If he figures out who you are, he could come looking for us."

Dee sighed. She could see his point, but it felt wrong to do *nothing.*

Suddenly Mason grabbed her arm and pointed. "Look."

She'd forgotten about the eggs. Now she saw that the bag was full of steam and she could hear popping noises from inside. She jumped to her feet and hugged Mason. "Is there anything you can't do?"

He tilted her chin up so he could look into her eyes. "There's at least one thing I can't do. I can't tell you how sorry I was to leave you that day after the EMP. But once I found out how serious it was, I couldn't leave Sammy and my mom on their own."

"But you could leave me?" Dee knew she wasn't being fair but she didn't care. "You should have just told me, I would have understood. You guys could have stayed with us." She stepped back and crossed her arms.

Mason put his hands in his pockets and half turned away, but Dee heard him say, "If I could go back I'd do it different. I'd do it all different." Then he walked away and the only sound Dee could hear was the sizzle of eggs in the sunlight.

CHAPTER SIXTEEN

As summer faded to fall, it seemed to Dee that as soon as one crop or plant was harvested and preserved, another ripened and had to be dealt with. She had never worked so hard in her life. She woke up before dawn every morning, still filthy and exhausted from the previous day. Her morning cup of coffee did little to wake or cheer her up, and the boisterous Searle brothers didn't improve her irritable mood. They were there every morning, full of energy and cracking jokes. She would have guessed it was a boy thing, but Mason looked as cross as she felt.

Mason might not have been a morning person or much of a farmer, but he more than made up for it by being a handyman. He made it his personal mission to get as much of the old farm machinery working as possible. The farm had belonged to Grandpa's family for several generations and they saved everything. An old train car sat abandoned in a small field behind the house, and this was the central location for most of the unwanted equipment. Around it were rusty tractors and trucks with tall grass growing up through the engines. Sammy loved to play there, pretending to drive or climbing on the vehicles like a jungle gym while Jasper barked and ran around below.

One morning Grandpa and Mason took a gas lantern and walked out to the old train car together. Grandpa explained the use of each antique while Mason inspected them and took notes. More than anything, Grandpa was worried about feeding the animals over the winter. Their primary feed was hay, which grew in fields around the house, and as long as it was kept fertilized and got enough water, he could cut it a few times over the summer and get enough to feed his animals.

In the distant past, they'd cut, raked, and baled the hay on the farm with their own equipment, but more recently it made sense financially to hire a crew with high-end equipment to get the job done quickly and cheaply. This year it would be up to Dee, Mason, and the three Searle boys to put up enough hay to get the animals through the winter. In the future, with some planning, they could let the animals graze through the winter, but Grandpa said he didn't have winter cover crops planted. This year their only choice was to get the hay harvested or the animals would probably starve. Dee didn't want to think about what would happen to her and Grandpa without the animals.

Hyrum experimented with an old scythe for a few hours and claimed it wouldn't be possible to cut enough hay by hand. They only had one scythe and even if they took turns and cut quickly they couldn't harvest enough for the winter. Grandpa fretted until Dee insisted he stay inside and let them handle it.

His health had improved since he started taking a mixture of cayenne and water every day, but she didn't think he'd ever get back to where he was before the attack. He moved like an old man now—slow and deliberate. Dee was sure he was in pain. She worried the stress of the harvest would be too much for him.

Over the years the old equipment had fallen into disrepair, and the first piece of machinery Mason got working was an antique mower. When he hitched it up behind the small tractor everyone came along to watch. Dee inspected it but was baffled by how it worked. It wasn't until they started mowing that she understood. As it rolled along behind the tractor, the wheels turned a gear in the center that moved a cutting blade back and forth. The trial run was a success, and everyone cheered.

Dee had no idea so many factors had to be considered when harvesting hay. Grandpa had to check the crop to make sure it was dry enough. He said if it rained while the cut hay was curing on the ground it could mold. It was getting late in the season, and as soon as the mower was ready they began cutting. The little mower wasn't very wide and it took a lot of passes to cut the whole field. They also had to make frequent stops to clean out the blades when they got jammed, but it was a huge improvement over cutting the whole thing by hand.

Dee worried about how much fuel it took to run the tractor back and forth over the field so many times, but Grandpa said gas didn't keep forever. His big tank of gas would start breaking down in a few months anyway, so they'd be best off using it while they had it. Dee didn't want to think about what they'd do when the gas ran out or spoiled.

After the cut hay sat out on the field for a day, Grandpa said it was time to gather it up. He had an old farm rake that attached to the tractor. It was a lot wider than the mower and was basically just a big pair of wheels and curved metal teeth. The teeth dragged across the ground behind the truck and pulled the cut grass to the edge of the field.

Grandpa said there was no way they'd be able to bale the hay, so he and Mason discussed how to keep it dry over the winter. In the end, Dee and the boys piled the hay on a base of wooden pallets. Using two-by-fours as supports, they made the haystacks as high as they could, trampling them down frequently to compact them. They secured big tarps over the haystacks, and Grandpa said it was as fine a job as he'd ever seen. When they had finished cutting and stacking all the hay, he went into his room for a while, and when he came out his eyes and nose were red. After that, Dee noticed he seemed more relaxed.

*

As much work as it was, Dee considered the garden a miracle. She'd never grown anything, and the idea of being able to pick and eat fresh produce from your own yard was miraculous to her. What she hadn't anticipated was how much work it would take to preserve all of the garden's bounty.

The tomatoes were the first to be ready, and once they started to ripen it seemed like they wouldn't stop. Dee and Sammy picked a box of ripe tomatoes every week and took them up to the Searle house, where Sammy and five-year-old Katy played while Dee and Angela worked. Grandpa said they'd always canned a lot of their own food, so he had boxes of canning jars and rings in storage. Angela said she had enough lids for ten families, and she was happy to share.

They ended up stewing most of the tomatoes, which Angela said was the easiest and most versatile method. This required washing the tomatoes and then cooking them briefly in boiling water until the skins cracked and peeled off. They cut the tomatoes into bite-sized chunks and boiled them with salt, pepper and a little sugar for about ten minutes. When they were done, they were poured into the clean canning jars and set to boil in two large canning pots Angela placed on a double-burner camp stove in the backyard. She said even when they had electricity she always did it this way because it was cooler than standing in a steaming, hot kitchen.

Lining up the processed jars of tomatoes and hearing the lids making popping noises as they sealed was one of the most satisfying experiences of Dee's life. She went home tired and content, and Grandpa served poached eggs in stewed tomatoes for dinner that night. Later in the season she learned how to make tomato sauce with a hand strainer and salsa with the onions, peppers, and garlic that were now ripening in the garden. The salsa even brightened up their old standby meal of scrambled eggs.

While Dee canned peaches, peas, green beans, and beets, the boys were busy in the fields. Under Grandpa's direction they brought in three truckloads of corn that they shucked and stored in an old corncrib, once they'd cleaned it out and repaired it. After they picked as many ears of corn as they could see, the cows were turned loose in the field to find the rest and eat the corn stalks.

Feed corn was a lot different from the sweet white corn Dee was used to eating back in Maryland. The kernels were thicker and tougher, but still delicious when eaten with plenty of salt and homemade butter.

On Sundays the Searles didn't normally come over to do chores, so Dee was surprised one Sunday afternoon when Jeremiah knocked on the door and invited them to come out for a picnic. It was too far for Grandpa to walk, but Dee, Mason, and Sammy were excited at the prospect of an outing. All of the Searles were there except Hyrum, who was finishing a book and said he'd head over after he finished. Sammy insisted on bringing Jasper, who ran circles around the whole group while they walked, as though trying to round them up.

The picnic area turned out to be the place where she had found Hyrum fishing. Apparently it was a favorite spot with the family. It was a warm autumn day and the sunlight filtering through the changing leaves created dappled patterns of light on the picnic blanket.

Angela provided a loaf of freshly baked bread and a container of spreadable cheese she'd made herself, cold grilled potato wedges, and a small can of olives as a treat. Dee brought a jar of home-canned pickles, celery spread with peanut butter, and the inevitable eggs—hard-boiled today.

While they ate, the boys talked about the work on the farm and speculated about how they could get some baby pigs to raise in the spring. Dee joined in the conversation now and then, but was mostly content to quietly enjoy the companionship of family and friends.

She tried to remember whether her family had ever spent time together like this before Jacob died and it made her a little melancholy to admit to herself that they hadn't. They loved each other, but talking and just being together wasn't something they did.

Dee's reflections were broken by laughter, and she looked over at Sammy, Katy, and Jasper. All three of their faces were covered in peanut butter from licking it out of the celery. "Some things will never change," she giggled as she eyed the stripped celery stalks, showing not a single nibble.

After the picnic was cleaned up, Angela sat under a tree and read a book while the children threw rocks in the stream. Jeremiah and Joseph went to look for the so-called bear cave, and Mason and Dee were left on the picnic blanket in the patchy sunlight.

"You're turning out to be quite the cook," said Mason, opening a pocketknife and whittling a stick he'd picked up. "Those eggs were hard-boiled to perfection."

"Ha-ha," she said, pushing against him with her shoulder. "You wouldn't be laughing if you'd been here before I started cooking lessons. It's really too bad you missed the great Fish Fry Debacle." Dee looked up suspiciously as Angela made a half-choked sound behind her book.

"See?" she told Mason. "The legend has already become part of oral tradition in Lookout Falls."

"Well, now you have to tell me. Maybe I can set the saga to music."

"You'd have to figure out something that rhymes with powdered sugar."

"Powdered sugar?" Mason's eyebrows shot up. "For a fish fry?"

"Oh, please. Don't tell me you've never confused powdered sugar and flour."

"Oh, um, yeah. I confuse them all the time. Twice yesterday." His eyes twinkled. "Just tell me one thing. Who discovered the mistake first? You or your grandpa?"

Dee thought back to the look on Grandpa's face when he'd put the first bite into his mouth. "He really took one for the team that time," she said, trying to keep a straight face.

Katy and Sammy were decorating Jasper's white ruff with a chain of braided grass. He sat patiently while they groomed him, but Dee saw him yawn nervously and look for an opportunity to escape. None presented itself, so he gave a sigh and lay down.

"You know what I miss?" said Mason. "Music. Mostly my iPod, but at this point I'd take golden oldies on one of those old-fashioned record players with the big horns." He turned and teased Angela. "Did you ever have one of those gramophone things, Mrs. Searle?"

Angela calmly turned a page in her book. "I'm too old for those new-fangled music players, sorry."

Dee smothered a laugh. "What kind of music did you used to listen to?" she asked Mason, expecting him to name some bluegrass or country bands.

"Have you ever heard of Collective Soul? My mom liked them a lot. We drove down to Spokane once to see them play at the county fair."

Dee tried to think if she knew any Collective Soul songs. "Didn't they have one called *Shine*?"

"Yep, that's their big one. Lately I've had a different one stuck in my head. It's called *The World I Know*. I bet you know it. Tell me if you recognize this." Mason sat up and began to sing.

Mason's voice filled the sunny clearing with a warm richness. Dee felt like she could drift away on the sound, and even Angela set her book aside and closed her eyes.

When he finished, Mason said, "Doesn't it seem to fit? My life is so different from what I thought it would be. Sometimes I don't know if I should laugh or cry."

Dee thought about everything he'd been through and laid her head on his shoulder. He put an arm around her and continued. "When I'm around you everything's better. I wouldn't be here if it wasn't for you."

"It's not ever going to be the same again, though, is it?"

"I don't know if I'd want it to be."

She tilted her head up to look at him. He was gazing at her intently, and for a moment she wondered if he was going to kiss her. Instead he reached for her hand and clipped his emergency bracelet around her wrist.

"Is that okay?" he asked. "Would you want to wear my wrist-band? I'm sorry it's not fancier."

Dee thought her heart would melt. She twisted the paracord around her wrist and thought it was the sweetest thing anyone had ever given her. She was just about to say thank you when she realized she couldn't hear the kids any more. Then a child's scream pierced the air, followed by Jasper's frenzied barking.

Angela, Mason, and Dee all jumped to their feet and raced toward the sound. Just a few steps into the woods a terrifying scene was poised to play out in front of them. Katy and Sammy stood perfectly still on a deer trail, and less than twelve feet away a huge mountain lion crouched, ready to pounce.

CHAPTER SEVENTEEN

Jasper was on the trail between the children and the big cat, lunging at it and barking for all he was worth. Blood dripped from his muzzle where he'd already been the victim of the mountain lion's sharp claws.

Mason had a branch in his hand, and Dee realized he'd torn it right off a tree. He and Angela quickly stepped between the children and the beast, adding a layer of protection. Jasper continued to try to drive off the animal. When he got too close it struck at him again, swift as lightning. The brave dog yelped as the force of the powerful paw knocked him to one side.

Angela had her hands up in front of her face like claws, and Mason slashed the air with the tree branch. They both yelled and growled like animals. Jasper struggled to regain his feet, barking and refusing to take his eyes off the enemy.

Finally, the mountain lion took a step backward. Mason advanced on it with another great swing of his club, and the big cat turned and ran into the trees. Angela reached to gather the children to her, but Sammy squirmed away and ran to Jasper.

Jasper tried to limp toward the little boy, but couldn't manage it. He stood on the trail, face scratched and left side matted with blood. He gave a feeble wag of his tail when the child reached him, but his strength was quickly draining and he laid down on the trail.

"Oh no—not Jasper," whispered Dee, hand to her mouth. Then she felt a surge of adrenaline. "We've got to get him home to Grandpa. He'll know what to do."

Jeremiah and Joseph were back, and they quickly packed up their site while Dee assessed the dog. "Those cuts on his side are pretty bad," she said. "We need something to stop the bleeding."

No sooner had she said the words than Sammy had his shirt off and pressed it into her hands. "Here, he can have this."

Dee took the small, threadbare T-shirt and folded it into a soft bandage, which she pressed firmly against the dog's side, and then she and Mason wrapped him up in the large quilt they'd used as a picnic blanket. Angela was anxious to get out of the area in case the big cat came back, so with Mason in the lead carrying Jasper they all hurried along the trail back home.

Jeremiah and Joseph ran ahead to tell Grandpa they were coming. Sammy stayed with Mason, whispering encouraging words to Jasper. At the farm, Grandpa was already waiting in the clinic when they got there, standing in the open doorway and motioning for Mason to bring in the dog.

Dee hadn't been inside the clinic before. It was a converted shed that was partitioned into three areas. There was a tiny reception area at the front with a desk and two chairs where people could wait, and at the back was a storage room with three animal crates on one wall across from shelves stacked with medical equipment and medicine. A small reach-in refrigerator stood in the corner.

Between the reception area and the storage area was a tiny exam room with a metal table and a window with sunlight streaming in. This was where Grandpa examined Jasper. His eyebrows were drawn down and his mouth was set in a grim line. "Dee, I'm gonna need an extra set of hands. Think you can handle it without passing out?"

Dee nodded, not entirely sure.

"All right, the rest of you need to get back on up to the house and out of my way." He spoke sternly but his voice softened when he saw Sammy stroking Jasper's head. "You, too, son. You can come back and see him in a little while."

After Mason led the sobbing boy out of the room, Dee helped Grandpa tend to Jasper's injuries. After they shaved the fur from his side, her heart sank as she saw how deep the cuts were.

They were using a local anesthetic, so Jasper was awake for the whole thing. He lay quietly on the table and seemed very small to Dee. She looked him in the eyes and told him he was a good dog, then held him still while Grandpa began the long process of stitching up his wounds.

When Grandpa finished, Dee helped him into the house and he sat in his recliner near the woodstove and watched as Mason helped Sammy make a soft bed of blankets for Jasper. Hyrum, who had come down to the house to join them for supper, carried the dog inside and put him on the bed near the fire. Grandpa told them all that the scratches were deep, but hadn't damaged any of Jasper's internal organs, and if they kept the wound clean and free of infection he had a really good chance of survival.

At that moment there was a knock on the door. Jasper made a feeble attempt at a bark, and Mason, Hyrum, and Dee jumped to their feet. Angela and Grandpa exchanged a nervous glance and then Grandpa went to the closet for his shotgun. He motioned for Hyrum to open the door and stood to one side with the gun ready. Mason had a baseball bat in hand and he went to stand by the window.

Hyrum opened the door a crack and peered out, then opened it wide. "It's Mr. Mortimer," he said in a relieved tone. To Dee, he explained, "He's our mailman."

Grandpa greeted the thin, balding man with a firm handshake. "Come on in, Morty. It's good to see you."

Dee saw that his postal uniform hung loosely on him, and she guessed he'd once been quite a bit larger. She'd lost weight herself. She wasn't rail-thin like Mason and Sammy, but her only pair of jeans had once been snug and now she needed a belt to keep them from falling down.

While the mailman made himself comfortable by the fire, Dee brewed him some coffee. As the smell wafted into the room, Mr. Mortimer sat up straight and sniffed the air. "Don't tell me you folks still have coffee." When Dee brought him a cup of the hot drink and offered him cream or sugar, he pretended to swoon and said, "I think I've died and gone to heaven."

"What's the word, Morty?" said Grandpa. "We check the radio every night for news but there's never a peep. Is anyone still out there?"

"It's not good, Milton," he replied with a glance at the children.

Angela told Joseph to take the two younger children upstairs and keep them busy with a puzzle. Once they left, Morty went on in a subdued voice.

"More than a third of the folks in town are dead, and more dying every day."

"I was afraid of that," said Grandpa in a grim tone. "These kids were there a couple of weeks after the power went out and it was already bad."

"I believe it," said Morty. "It started with the water. It quit running the first day and people just drank whatever they could find. Wasn't long before they got the runs and whatever else you get from drinking fouled water."

"Probably cholera," Grandpa said.

Morty nodded. "There ain't no one hauling trash any more, no water, and no sewage. A lot of people are too sick to even bury their dead. The streets are a disgusting mess and it's spreading through what water there is, so . . . you can imagine," he finished.

"Is anyone in charge down there?" asked Angela.

"Not so much anymore. The police and fire departments teamed up at first. Sheriff and his folks patrolled the streets while the fire chief kept up roadblocks. It didn't help, though."

"What do you mean?"

"Even with the curfews and roadblocks, people were still robbing each other, stealing food for themselves and their kids. Desperation changes people. It wouldn't have gotten so bad so fast, but early on a gang formed up. They broke into homes and stole whatever food they could get their hands on. If someone was lucky enough to pull through the sickness, chances are they woke up just to starve."

"Who would do that?" said Angela, horrified.

"I wish I knew," said Morty, "but you folks need to be ready to defend yourselves. I've heard they're raiding houses and farms outside town now, too."

"How many are there?" asked Mason. "And how much firepower are they packing?"

"That's the strange thing," said the mail carrier. "I don't think they ever just outright attack, and they ain't hardly killed no one, either. They sneak in, take the food, and sneak out. Somehow they always know right where to look for it."

Mason interrupted. "Is my stepdad still alive?"

Morty nodded. "I don't know what we would've done without Hank. He's been going around to folks, teaching them to boil water, giving out food and medicine when he can. I've seen him walking the streets at night trying to enforce the curfew on his own. He gives folks hope."

Mason snorted and all eyes turned to him. "Are you sure we're talking about the same guy? Sounds like he's pulled the wool over everyone's eyes. You know he was stealing food from people, right? If he's helping out, that must mean there's something in it for him."

"I heard about the trouble you had with him a few months back, but he's not the same man. He really cares about people." Morty seemed sincere.

"He can play nice when he has to, but it won't last. All he cares about is himself." Mason's face was a cold mask.

"So what brings you out here?" Grandpa asked, changing the subject. "Don't tell me it's all bad news."

"Nope, you'll like this. I got word up from Spokane that they're trying to get the mail started again. It's going to be a lot slower than it used to be, obviously. The term *snail mail* finally fits." Morty chuckled at his own joke, then continued. "No packages, nothing heavy. No stamps, either," he added, and his eyes gleamed. "But if you have something to donate to your mail carrier, it's appreciated."

"Of course, of course, Morty," said Grandpa. "I would have invited you to stay for supper anyway. I hope you will. That'll give us a few minutes to write some letters, and then we'll send you on your way with a full stomach and something for the road."

The mailman sniffed the air and said, "Don't mind if I do. I haven't smelled something that good in I don't know how long. If I don't miss my guess, that's chicken noodle soup."

Angela got up to check the pot that was simmering on the woodstove, and Morty joined her and offered to stir it. "I can't remember the last time I saw noodles, or chicken for that matter." He brought the spoon to his lips and took a sip. "I could die happy now," he said, putting the spoon back into the pot, "and I've got just the thing to go with it. When I told Hank I was going out to let folks know about the mail, he gave me a sack of flour and told me to make something I could take around to people." Morty opened a bag and pulled out some flat, round disks. "So I made crackers.

Nothing but flour and water." Grandpa made a sound of dismay and Morty added, "*Clean* water. I boiled it myself."

Mason looked ready to object, but Angela put a hand on his arm and said, "They'll be perfect with the soup, like matzo. Jeremiah, go set an extra place at the table for Mr. Mortimer, and we'll eat."

"He can have my spot," came a little voice. It was Sammy. "Can I just stay here with Jasper for dinner? I'm not very hungry."

Angela looked at Mason to see if he minded and then nodded. "Sure, honey. I know he'll like that."

The sight of the little boy keeping watch over his wounded dog was enough to break Dee's heart. Sammy'd had enough loss in his life. She willed Jasper to get better.

At dinner, Morty ladled bowls of soup for everyone while he explained how the temporary mail would work. "We're counting on people to help us right now. Say, for example, you decide you're going to leave town—we'd want you to stop by the post office first and tell us where you're going. If we've got letters that need to go that way we'll give you a bag and you can take them. Hopefully as people pass through town they'll have letters for us that they'll bring by the post office, and I'll take them around as often as I can. We've got a few dedicated letter carriers willing to make the long haul, but that's a lot to ask. Most of us want to stay closer to home."

"Aren't you worried about security?" asked Grandpa.

"Some," answered Morty, and then he loudly slurped a noodle and smacked his lips. "Hank's offered me whatever protection he can manage."

"Seems risky to me," said Grandpa.

"It's a good idea," said Angela. She hadn't taken a bowl of soup for herself. Instead, she was busy writing. Dee was sure she was writing to her oldest son. Dee set her own bowl aside when she was done and tore a page out of a notebook. She wanted to write to her parents, but what could she say?

She glanced at Mr. Mortimer to see if he was ready to leave, but he was busily refilling his bowl to the brim and asking Grandpa about the farm and the animals. Dee sat on the couch and looked again at the blank page in front of her. As months passed with no sign of her parents, Dee had begun to give up hope. She told herself it would be better not to expect them at all, so if they never came it wouldn't hurt as much. She had so much to tell them, but putting anything down on paper felt like hoping for too much.

Dee looked up as Hyrum sat next to her. "What's wrong?" he whispered, looking at her blank sheet of paper.

"What if I write this and they never get it?" she said. "I don't even know where to address it."

Hyrum thought for a minute and then said, "Do you remember that scene in the third *Indiana Jones* movie? Where he's standing in front of a bottomless pit, and to save his dad he has to cross it?"

For once, Dee knew which movie Hyrum was talking about. She could see it in her mind. Harrison Ford with his leg held out stiffly in front of him, looking like he was about to step off the edge of a cliff. Prepared to take—

"A leap of faith," she said out loud.

"Sometimes you've just got to take the leap." Hyrum smiled at her and Dee felt a warm reassurance as he added, "It's going to be okay." And somehow, for a minute, she believed him. She picked up her pencil and began to write.

CHAPTER EIGHTEEN

After Morty left with their letters and a dozen eggs packed carefully in dry grass, Grandpa and Angela washed the dishes while the kids played charades in the living room. Jeremiah had them all in stitches doing an impression of Mr. Mortimer licking his soup bowl clean.

Dee wandered into the kitchen to offer to help and inadvertently overheard a conversation.

"I don't like it, Angela. He's been in the house. He knows how we're set for winter." Grandpa took a bowl from her and dried it before putting it in the cupboard.

"I think we should give him the benefit of the doubt. He's a good man. We can't suspect him just because he looked hungry."

"We have to suspect him," said Grandpa. "We've got young'uns here that need protecting, and Morty said it himself—hunger changes people."

"All right, so he's hungry. That doesn't mean he's involved with those thieves." Angela scrubbed fiercely at a bowl that already looked clean. "Plus, if he was that hungry he wouldn't have shared his food with us."

"I completely agree, but right now there's no way to know, and we need to do what's best for the kids."

Angela sighed and leaned against the sink, shoulders slumped. "Fine, I'll tell the boys we're moving in for the winter. We'll bring our things tomorrow."

*

The next day, as soon as Dee had a chance, she got Hyrum and Mason together and told them what she'd overheard about Mr. Mortimer.

"Morty? One of the bad guys?" said Hyrum, doubt clear in his eyes. "That sounds like paranoia."

"Think about it, though," said Mason. "He's the perfect choice for a lead man. People know him and trust him. *We* let him in, didn't we? Now he knows the layout of the house, and he knows we've got food and livestock and guns."

"What if he *is* with them? Our storage would be a huge score for a group like that, and so would the animals. How do we protect them?" asked Dee.

The three put their heads together and came up with some ideas. After they presented them to Grandpa and Angela a few modifications were made and then the teens got to work.

The first thing they did was prepare a place to hide the bulk of their supplies. There was already quite a bit of food in the house, and with the addition of the Searles and their food, it was imperative they get it out of sight. Dee had never noticed, but under the mat in the pantry was a trapdoor leading to a dank and musty cellar.

"This is perfect," breathed Mason, shining his flashlight around the space. "No one will ever suspect this room is down here." The walls of the windowless room were lined with old wooden shelves. Mason inspected them and pronounced them solid, so after they cleaned them up they started bringing the food down into storage.

Hyrum and his brothers made multiple trips, lugging huge canisters into the house in a strange procession of things like hard red wheat, dehydrated apples, nonfat dried milk, Potato Pearls, and more.

Dee watched in amazement and finally stopped Hyrum as he walked by with a five-gallon bucket labeled macaroni. "Is your mom a little crazy? Who has twenty pounds of macaroni?"

Hyrum grinned good-naturedly. "Was Noah a little crazy when he built the ark? Guess who was laughing when the rain started?"

"Glad to have you on board, Noah."

They left just enough food in the pantry to make it seem like it was all they had, but the majority of their supplies was now hidden beneath the trapdoor.

Mason wanted to rig up some kind of alarm so they'd know if someone brought a vehicle down the lane. He spent several days foraging through Grandpa's house and the Searles' to come up with the materials he needed. Dee thought he looked happier than a little boy on Christmas morning when she found a spool of insulated wire in a shoe box under the kitchen sink. He swung her around until she was dizzy and then kissed her on the cheek. "You're an angel," he declared.

Mason strung the wire from the house as far as it would reach along the side of the lane and then created a trip wire that stretched across the lane. If someone or something crossed the trip wire it pulled a slender piece of wood out from between an alligator clip with wires wrapped around both handles. The wires, which ran to a battery, would connect, and the battery would send a signal down the length of the wire to the house, where it would ring the doorbell.

They were all relieved when Mason finally got the alarm system working properly. It was nice knowing it would be harder for someone to sneak up on them in the night, but everyone was especially glad the development phase was over and Mason's system was no longer ringing the doorbell constantly and sending the injured dog into crazy barking sprees.

Jasper was also happy to have the Searles living with them. He was recovering quickly, but Grandpa said too much running around would be bad for him. Grandpa threatened to shut the excited dog in the clinic until he calmed down, so Sammy held him tightly while Angela cleaned out the upstairs bedrooms and moved her family in.

Dee got to keep her room, Angela and Katy shared a room, and Sammy, Jeremiah, and Joseph were all in the third. Although the fourth bedroom had beds for Hyrum and Mason, they talked the adults into letting them sleep out in the barn to keep an eye on the animals.

"It's all right for now," said Grandpa, "and we can see how it goes."

*

Even though the house felt crowded and loud, there were a lot of benefits of having the Searles living with them. From Dee's point of view, her chore load was quite a bit easier now that she had Angela and her boys to share the big jobs like cooking, cleaning, and especially laundry.

It turned out that the dishwasher wasn't the appliance Dee missed most—it was the washing machine. When she'd been alive, Grandma had decorated the laundry room with an old washboard and basin. Dee wondered why anyone that had used those items would ever view them as decorative. "More like torturous," she muttered to herself as she scrubbed dirty clothes up and down over the bumpy surface of the washboard.

Mason had hinted at an idea for a washing machine type of invention, but when she saw that the prototype consisted of a bucket and a plunger, Dee sent him away. She refused to wash clothes with something that had been in the toilet.

Another thing Dee considered a benefit was getting to share in a Searle family tradition they called "family home evening." Every Monday night they all gathered in the living room and played games and spent time together. Each week different members of the family took on different assignments, which included saying the opening and closing prayers, preparing a short lesson, choosing a game, and making a treat. Dee had to work not to laugh the night Katy prayed, "Please bless that next week it will be Mom's turn to make the treat 'cause she's the only one that knows how to make brownies."

The thing Dee enjoyed most about having the Searles around though was the music, and she knew Mason agreed. Each of the Searle kids played an instrument, and Angela insisted they continue practicing. Hyrum played the guitar, Jeremiah played the violin, and Joseph could play the piano but preferred the harmonica. Even Katy had a set of bells upon which she was learning to play simple melodies. It wasn't unusual after dinner to have one or several of the Searles play, while anyone could join in singing.

Somehow, Dee found that sharing in the closeness of the family helped soothe her own ache at the loss of her brother, and even to a certain extent, her fears and worries about her parents. She wished they could be there, and see what a happy family was like from the inside.

Thanksgiving that year was unlike any Dee had ever had. On a typical Thanksgiving, her father spent the day engrossed in one football game after another, while her mom went over newspaper and online ads, looking for bargains and trying to score lightning deals on Amazon. Dee and Jacob typically watched the parade together on TV and then spent most of the day texting with their friends or playing computer games in their rooms. Dinner was a brief affair, which involved her mom reheating a prepackaged Thanksgiving meal. They ate together in the mostly unused dining room and made small talk. Dee remembered looking forward to the holiday. Her whole family was at home, and even if they spent the day doing their own things, at least they were there together.

This year, she experienced a completely different kind of Thanksgiving Day. Angela said that for one day they wouldn't be careful about food rationing and would have a real feast. Mason and Hyrum had gone hunting and actually found a wild turkey. It was small and lean, but they were very proud. The women had done much of the cooking in the days leading up to the holiday, so by Thursday they already had an apple pie and a pumpkin pie, a mountain of rolls, fresh butter and jam, and a sweet potato casserole waiting to go into the oven. The mashed potatoes and gravy had to be done right at the end, so while the bird cooked, they all hung out together.

They looked through photo albums and reminisced about family members who weren't there, and they told funny stories about things they remembered. It was emotional at times, especially for Mason and Sammy, who had just lost their mom, but it felt good to Dee to talk about loved ones in a familiar way instead of carefully avoiding any mention of them.

Angela found a brown paper bag and cut out a turkey head and body in the shape of a bowling pin, and then everyone traced their hands and colored them to be the turkey's tail feathers. On each finger, they wrote what they were thankful for and cut them out. After the project was assembled on the wall in the kitchen, Dee was both amused and touched to read what everyone was thankful for. Some of her favorites included:

Jasper
the cattle guard
having enough to eat
being rescued
fresh milk
football
Angela because she is nice (from Sammy)
warm house
forever families
no school
Grandpa
big woodpile
finding the truck
Jesus
the pump
toilet paper—wish we had some!
being alive

Dinner was a joyous feast and they all ate until they were stuffed. After dinner there were a lot of leftovers and Dee wished aloud they had someone to share with. Angela asked if she knew anyone who would be grateful for the food. Dee thought immediately of Courtney and her three little girls. They'd been on her mind lately, and Dee was worried they might be getting low on supplies. Grandpa and Angela said as long as Mason and Hyrum went with her she could take the leftovers and a small care package to the family.

Dee carefully packed fresh eggs and milk, along with some rice, beans, flour, and cornmeal. Then she added a coloring book, along with some markers and a candy bar. Her heart was light as they left the house and headed for Courtney's.

It was only a few miles, so the three teens walked. As they neared the house Dee was happy to see plant stalks in the frozen garden. Maybe Courtney had been able to grow some vegetables, after all.

Dee's mood changed as she looked more closely at the house. Neglect gave it an ominous air.

"I don't see any smoke from the chimney," said Hyrum, stepping back to look.

"Do you think they left?" asked Mason.

"Maybe," said Dee, unsure now. "Maybe her husband came back and they decided to leave."

"I've got a bad feeling about this," said Hyrum. Dee silently agreed.

She knocked on the door loudly and called, "Courtney, it's Dee. I watched your girls once, remember? I've got something for you."

After a long pause, they heard the lock turn and the door opened a crack. "Now's not a good time," said a shaky voice.

"Hi, Courtney, it's me. Can we come in? It's Thanksgiving and I've brought you something. Look." Dee held up one of the eggs.

The door opened wider and the afternoon light shone fully on the young woman. Dee stared. She barely recognized Courtney. Greasy blond hair was pulled back in a scraggly ponytail. Clothes hung from her emaciated body. Heavy shadows bruised the skin under her sunken eyes.

"Oh no, Courtney, what happened? Are you okay?" Dee offered her an arm. "Let me help you back inside."

"Just you," said Courtney in a raspy voice. "I don't know these other two."

Mason looked doubtful and Hyrum said, "Are you sure that's a good idea?"

When Dee assured them she'd just be a few minutes, Hyrum and Mason agreed to wait outside and she helped Courtney slowly to the couch. Dee thought her legs might give out at any moment.

"What happened? You look like you've had a rough time," said Dee.

"You have no idea," said Courtney.

"Tell me about it." Dee sat on the edge of the seat, her eyes fixed on the young woman.

"The girls got sick. I think they might have been drinking the water in the ditch. I'm not sure." Courtney raised skeletal shoulders in a shrug. "But they got me sick, too."

"Are they okay?" asked Dee. She looked around and realized she hadn't seen or heard any of the children. A feeling of dread started to creep over her.

"They got better before I did," said Courtney. "I'd been giving them more food, you know, so they were stronger than I was. When my fever broke I could hear them crying. I crawled out of my room and found them scared and hiding. They said bad men came into the house while I was sick and took the food."

"What?" gasped Dee. "They just took it?"

"The girls let them in thinking they were here to help, but they came in and took every last bit of food we had. Those animals took it while the girls watched." Courtney's voice was hard. "They knew there were children here and they took it anyway. All they left us was a box of breakfast bars."

"How long ago was that?" asked Dee.

Courtney shrugged her thin shoulders again.

Dee put a hand on Courtney's leg. "Where is Sarah now?"

"In bed," said Courtney. "They're all safe in their beds."

It was too early for bedtime.

"I'm just going to check on them," said Dee.

She went to Beth's toddler bed first and pulled back the covers but she already knew what she would find. Beth was dressed in her favorite pajama sleeper, the one with the kittens, and her eyes were closed.

She was dead.

"Sleep now, little baby," whispered Dee, tucking the covers back around the small corpse.

She checked the other two beds and found the same thing. Both young girls wore clean pajamas and were tucked into perfectly made beds with clean sheets. Dee straightened up and considered. The girls were small, but they weren't wasted away by hunger like Courtney was.

Dee walked slowly back to the living room, her heart heavy.

"Aren't they peaceful?" sighed Courtney. "My little angels. They would have suffered, you know."

"What do you mean?" asked Dee. Horror clutched at her throat as an unthinkable idea began to take shape. "What do you mean they would have suffered?"

"I couldn't let them outlive me, Dee. All that time I'd been giving them more food. I thought that's what a good mother does—sacrifices for her children, but I had it wrong. I was going to die first and they would have been alone. This way they didn't have to suffer."

"They didn't have to die," said Dee, her voice rising. "You could have come to me! I would have helped you!"

"Look at me. I can barely get to the door. We never would have made it to your place."

Dee looked and knew she was right. "What about your neighbors?"

"What neighbors?" said Courtney in a flat voice.

"Then your husband. He could still be coming."

"He's dead. Morty came by bringing mail from Spokane and there was nothing from him. If he was alive he would have written."

Silence fell as Dee struggled with her emotions. She could hardly believe what she was hearing. Courtney was a good mom.

Good moms didn't do this . . . this thing. They took care of their kids. They protected them.

For a moment Dee thought about her own mom. She hadn't been able to protect her son from the car that killed him. In the days after his death she had been so small and lost, and during the long nights her sobs filled the emptiness of their house. Maybe moms couldn't always protect their kids, after all. Maybe they just did the best they could, and sometimes it wasn't enough.

Dee's horror at what Courtney had done was replaced by a deep, aching sorrow.

"Tell me about the girls," said Dee in a low voice. She didn't want to know, but she had to.

"We had a wonderful day that last day," said Courtney, with a smile in her voice as she remembered. "The girls drew pictures for me, and we played I Spy and did puzzles. They had a tea party and served each other their breakfast bars. They were so hungry they didn't taste the pills I mashed up and put inside. Afterward they told me their bellies didn't hurt anymore. Then I tucked them into their beds and sang songs and told them stories about someday, when we'll all be together again.

"After they fell asleep I watched them for the longest time in the candlelight. My sweet little angels. And then I . . ." Courtney's voice finally broke and she sobbed. "Oh Dee, they were my babies. What have I done?"

Dee sat next to Courtney and wrapped her arms around the fragile woman, holding her while she shook with agony.

When the young mother's sobs had quieted, Dee looked at her and said firmly, "Listen, Courtney. I'm going to send my friends back to Grandpa's to bring down the truck and I'm taking you home with me. We've got enough food for you . . ."

Courtney interrupted. "I can't leave my girls, Dee."

"We'll bring them," said Dee, wiping her eyes. "I know the perfect place. A clear little stream of bubbling water next to a big weeping willow and a field of wildflowers. They will love it, and you can visit them."

"You don't understand, Dee. I'm not going with you. I don't deserve it."

"What are you talking about?" Dee said. "If you stay here you'll die. There's no way I can just leave you here."

"That's what I want. It's what I deserve." Courtney reached out and took Dee's hand in her frail one. "Please just go. Let me dream about my little girls until I slip away."

Dee wiped angrily at her tears. If only she'd come a few days earlier. "I don't leave people behind, Courtney. Don't ask me to do it. I couldn't live with myself if I just left you here."

Courtney's eyes were huge in her face as she whispered, "I can't live with myself, either, not after what I've done."

*

Dee stumbled out of the house, past Mason and Hyrum, who were playing cards on the patio. "Hold on, Dee," said Mason, hurrying to catch up.

"What's the matter?" asked Hyrum.

When Dee got to the road she leaned over and vomited into the ditch. If she had come a week ago the little girls would still be alive, and now she'd left their mom to die, too. She couldn't do it. She would bring Angela to talk some sense into Courtney. Maybe together they'd have more luck.

Dee felt sick at the thought of how lucky she was, while children five miles down the road were starving. It wasn't supposed to be like this. She'd helped Courtney get food for her family. They should have had enough to last well into winter.

Whoever had robbed Courtney might as well have pointed a gun at her and her kids and pulled the trigger. Who would steal food out of the mouths of children? How many other families had this happened to? What kind of evil people did this? She was going to find out, and then she was going to put a stop to it.

CHAPTER NINETEEN

When Dee got home she went straight up to her room. Crying had given her a headache and she just wanted the day to be over, but once she was in bed she couldn't fall asleep. She kept thinking about Courtney. If she'd just waited and not given up hope the girls would still be alive. Then Dee tried to put herself in Courtney's shoes. If she was certain she was dying and there was no one left to take care of Sammy and Katy, what would she do?

It was impossible. Dee tossed and turned and finally fell into a restless sleep.

When she woke up a few hours later she still had a headache, but now her stomach hurt and she needed to use the bathroom right away. Afterward, she wrapped up tightly in her quilt but couldn't get warm. She felt her forehead and thought she had a fever. *I'm sick*, she realized grimly.

Once she realized she was sick, she couldn't get back to sleep. *Please let it just be me,* she silently prayed. But as she waited for morning she heard other feet cross the hallway to the bathroom, and then she heard a child crying in the night.

By the next morning, almost everyone was sick. Each had varying degrees of the same symptoms, which included headache, fever, vomiting and diarrhea, aches and pains, and weakness.

Dee came downstairs wrapped in a blanket with one of the bags she'd gotten at the grocery store. Angela looked through it and then hugged her fiercely. "Bless your heart, you got Tylenol."

Dee looked at the small bottle of pills doubtfully. It didn't seem like it would last very long if eight people all needed it. She opened her mouth to say that she'd skip her share so Katy could have it. Then she thought about Courtney and closed her mouth without speaking. They *all* had to get better.

The only two not showing symptoms were Angela and Sammy. Angela insisted that everyone needed to rest and save their strength for fighting the illness. She and Sammy would take over the chores as best they could. She made Hyrum and Mason stop sleeping in the barn until they felt better, and they shared the fourth bedroom upstairs.

Since almost no one in the house had any appetite Angela was spared much cooking. As the weather turned colder, the farm animals had stopped producing, so the chores were reduced on that count, too. Grandpa even suggested Angela get Jasper to help her take the cows out to the hay pasture and let them graze.

The woodpile was still high, but the laundry piled up quickly, and they were using a lot of water for disinfecting sheets and anything else the sick people came in contact with as well as for pouring into the toilets to make them flush.

Dee wanted to see Grandpa. Her limbs were weak and heavy, and it took a surprising amount of effort to get across the house to his room, but when she got there his sheets were crumpled and empty. She waited, thinking maybe he was in the bathroom, but he didn't return so she went looking for him.

She found him behind the desk in his office with a thick medical encyclopedia open in front of him. The pages were thin and yellow, and Grandpa had his glasses on to read the tiny print.

She leaned against the door. "Why aren't you in bed?"

"I'm trying to figure out what we've got," said Grandpa, peering over his glasses at her. "I expected cholera, but it doesn't fit. The diarrhea isn't severe enough."

Dee made a face. "That's really disgusting. And anyway, it seems pretty severe to me."

"Do you have a headache and a fever?" He rubbed his own temples. "Definitely not cholera. No fever with that."

Dee didn't think she could hold herself up anymore. "All right, I'm going to go rest for a few minutes. Let me know if you need anything." She didn't even make it upstairs. She got as far as the couch and decided to sit down for a minute, then fell asleep. Her sleep was fitful, and she woke up feeling like there was something she was forgetting. She knew it was important but she couldn't put her finger on it. Something about Courtney.

She got up on wobbly legs and managed to get to the kitchen. Angela was sitting at the table with her head on her arms.

"What's wrong?" Dee asked, alarmed at the woman's flushed cheeks.

Angela sat up and quickly wiped away tears. "Oh, hi, Maddie. What are you doing up? You should be resting."

"I was just wondering if there's something I could do to help." Dee clutched the door frame for support.

"Look at you, you can barely stand up. Let's get you back to the couch." Angela put an arm around Dee and helped her into the living room. Dee could feel the heat radiating from Angela's body.

"Are you okay? You feel hot."

"Don't you worry about anything except getting better. Sammy and I can take care of things around here."

Dee knew that she should stay up and help Angela, but her head was splitting and she slipped back into sleep as soon as she lay down.

She didn't know how long she'd slept when she awoke to the sound of Grandpa calling from his room. She tried to sit up and her vision swam. Dee swung her legs to the floor and closed her eyes to stop the room from spinning. Her head felt like it weighed a thousand pounds and was ready to roll off her shoulders and onto the floor. Angela must have heard him call; she could take care of it. Dee leaned forward and rested her head on her knees. *Come on, Angela*, she thought.

Grandpa called again and Dee knew she had to go to him. She tried to stand up, but the room tilted dangerously and she sat down quickly. It seemed cold. Was there a fire in the stove? She was having hot and cold chills and couldn't tell. Dee got down on her hands and knees and crawled toward Grandpa's room. Crawling didn't help her headache, but at least if she fell she wouldn't have far to go.

The floor stretched out endlessly in front of her. She'd never make it all the way to Grandpa's room. She set her sights on the front door instead. It was slow going, but she made it. When she got there she let herself rest for a moment before moving to the hallway. When she passed the bathroom she looked in and saw the bottle of Tylenol, so she stopped to take two for her head, thinking she needed more like fifty. Then she went on, stopping just inside his door, and tried to process the scene.

"Oh no," she breathed, crawling to where Angela had collapsed on the floor. She felt her face—she was burning up. Dee shook her. "Angela, wake up! You've got to get up."

Angela's eyes flew open and she cried out, "I'm coming, Katy!" She strained for a moment to sit up but then fell back to the floor. Dee didn't think Angela had even seen her. Her fever was so high she was delirious.

Grandpa was on his bed, looking down at the two of them. His thin hair was sweaty and plastered to his forehead and he shivered with chills. Dee looked helplessly up at him. "I don't know what to do. I can't move her."

He handed her a pillow and a blanket from the bed. "Just try to make her comfortable, and then I need you to do something."

After Dee did what she could to wrap Angela in the blanket, she wanted to lie down next to her and never get up, but Grandpa had a job for her.

"I think I know what we've got," he said. Dee noticed he had the big medical book open in bed next to him. "It's typhoid."

"As in typhoid fever?" she said. "Could I have . . . ? I'm so stupid. I must have caught it at Courtney's. She said they were sick." Dee didn't realize it was possible to feel even more miserable. This was all her fault.

"No, no, Maddie-girl, it wasn't you. It takes weeks before symptoms set in." He went on. "If I'm right, I've got something out in the clinic to treat it."

"Animal medicine?"

"Yes, we give animals some of the same antibiotics we use for ourselves. If we can get some of that into everyone, we should start getting better."

"And without it?"

Grandpa was silent.

Dee thought about how far it was to the clinic. "I don't know if I can make it."

"*I* know you can, Maddie." The belief in his eyes was unwavering and she knew she had to try.

He explained what she needed to look for and then reached over and handed her his cane. "It's magic, you know." Dee held it tightly by the glass ball on the end until it warmed under her hand.

The walk to the clinic was excruciatingly slow and gave Dee too much time to think. What if she couldn't find the right bottle? What if there wasn't enough? How would she get the kids to take it? How was she even going to get up the stairs? It seemed impossible.

One step at a time, she told herself. She watched her feet and concentrated on making them take a single step. Then one more, and another, and another. It was working. Before she knew it she was inside the clinic. She made herself take some more steps to the back room. He'd said the medicine was on the storage shelves in the kennel area.

There it was. It was a big white bottle like she'd expect to see behind the counter in a pharmacy. She shook it and almost laughed to feel all of the pills rolling inside. Opening it, she took two out and swallowed them dry before making her way back. She paused in the reception area and looked at the office chair behind the desk. Would it roll across concrete? It might, but she realized if she sat down in it she'd never want to get back up. She left it, and headed back to the house on her feet.

The walk back to the house was better. She had the cure in her hands, and she was determined to get it to everyone. Leaning heavily on Grandpa's cane and resting after every step, she made it up the front stairs of the patio.

She went to Grandpa's room first and woke him up. He was confused and called her Madeleine before he woke up completely and saw what she had. "That's my girl," he said. She helped him take two of the pills and then knelt beside Angela.

"Open the capsule and pour the powder under her tongue," said Grandpa.

Dee hesitated. "What if she's allergic?"

"I guess we'll find out."

*

It was quiet upstairs. Dee paused at the top of the steps to catch her breath and worry about what she'd find, but it wasn't too bad. Everyone was running a fever but they were all in their beds, most of them asleep. If they woke up she helped them take the medicine, and if they didn't she put it under their tongues. She found Sammy in bed with Mason. His little cheeks were flushed but he sat up and took the medicine when she showed him what to do.

Hyrum was awake and asked about his mom.

"I'm afraid she's come down with it, too," Dee said, handing him his dose.

"You need help, then," he said and tried to sit up.

Dee put a hand on his shoulder to stop him. "Maybe tomorrow. Just rest for now. I've got this."

He settled back down into bed and she was sure he was asleep before she left the room. In her own room, she sat on the bed and marveled at how good it felt to stop standing. Then she got into bed and fell asleep without another thought.

*

The antibiotics made a big difference for everyone but Angela. While the others were slowly improving, Angela's fever and delirium continued. It was difficult to get her to take the medicine, and impossible to get her to eat or drink more than just a few sips of water. Grandpa said they had to be patient and let it run its course because it was worse in some people than others. Dee saw from the haunted look in the eyes of her children that this was no comfort at all.

By now they'd moved her into Grandpa's bed and he was sleeping on the couch. They took turns sitting with her and keeping cool cloths on her forehead and neck. Tylenol worked to bring her fever down slightly, but it didn't control it, and Dee worried that she was cooking from the inside out. While she kept watch, Hyrum came into the room and knelt on the other side of the bed near Angela's head.

She saw that his hands shook and she didn't know whether it was from lingering weakness or fear for his mom. "I'm going to say a blessing over her to ask God to heal her."

Dee stood up. "I'll give you some time alone." She went into the next room and added a silent prayer on Angela's behalf. She was a mother to all of them, and Dee couldn't imagine life without her.

Angela's fever broke later that night. Grandpa said that the sickness had run its course and the antibiotics had finally kicked in. Dee watched as the Searle children crowded around their mother, laughing and crying and trying to hug her. Hyrum leaned over and kissed Angela's forehead. She smiled up at him weakly and put a hand on his cheek. "You remind me so much of your dad," she said before falling into a deep and restful sleep.

*

That night Dee had a hard time falling asleep—she couldn't stop thinking about Courtney. She'd planned to go back for her, but then they'd all gotten sick and now it was too late. Dee knew it was what the woman had wanted, but it didn't make Dee feel any better. When she finally did doze off she had a nightmare.

In the dream, it was pitch-black and she didn't know where she was. Maybe somewhere in the farmhouse. Then she heard a sound that chilled her—the squeak of the front door on its hinges.

Dee barely breathed. She told herself it was probably Mason or Hyrum coming in from checking on the cattle, but she knew the cows were grazing out in the pasture, and the boys were sleeping in the house.

Beams of several flashlights arced across the ceiling and Dee held her breath. It was the home invaders, she was sure. A wave of fury built up in her chest as she heard them walk into the kitchen and begin opening cupboard doors. She longed to leap up and confront them, punching and kicking and tearing them to pieces, but her dream self couldn't move.

Tears of frustration formed in her eyes. They were being robbed and there was nothing she could do about it. She listened closely. Had they found the trapdoor to the cellar? She couldn't tell. But she heard chickens squawking and Grandpa's truck engine roar to life. They would be left with nothing.

"Is that it?" a voice whispered.

"For now. We'll come back for the rest when they're gone."

Even in her dream Dee knew what the voice meant when it said, "when they're gone."

When they were dead.

She woke up in a cold sweat. The thieves were coming.

CHAPTER TWENTY

Grandpa, Dee, Hyrum, and Mason sat around the table in the sunny kitchen. They were in varying stages of recovery and all looked the worse for wear.

"What I don't understand is how they know which homes to target," said Hyrum. "I'm not sure we have enough information to form a pattern."

"Courtney said it happened to her, and Morty reported the same thing was happening to other families," Dee pointed out.

"Sammy said they broke into our house, too," added Mason. "Not sure if my mom was sick at the time, though."

"Let's just say for a minute that they do know," said Dee. "How is that even possible? They can't keep tabs on that many people."

"What if they know who to watch ahead of time?" said Grandpa thoughtfully.

"Like guessing which families will get sick based on where they live, or if their neighbors are sick?"

"No, I mean what if they are infecting them on purpose?"

Everyone fell silent. The idea was horrifying.

"That's terrorism," Hyrum said.

Grandpa nodded. "The incubation period of typhoid is two weeks, and then if you don't have the right medicine it can last four weeks or longer. That would give them a big window of opportunity."

Dee asked. "Wouldn't it be risky for them, going into contaminated houses?"

"Not if they're careful," said Grandpa. "Typhoid doesn't spread through the air. It has to be in the food or the water."

"But our water is clean, and none of us were sick or exposed. That doesn't make any sense. How did we get it?" said Mason. He got up and began to pace.

"Did you read about Typhoid Mary in history class?" asked Grandpa. The name sounded familiar and Dee tried to remember.

"Sure, I read a book about her," said Mason, and then he stopped dead in his tracks and turned to them. "She was a typhoid carrier, but she wasn't sick. She was a cook, and wherever she worked people got sick and died. They finally had to lock her up because she was such a threat."

"Morty. Didn't he help with the soup that night?" said Hyrum. "I don't remember him washing his hands."

Everyone fell quiet, thinking of the jolly mail carrier.

"Do you think he knows?" asked Dee finally.

"That's the question, now, isn't it?" said Grandpa. "He's been our mailman for as long as I can remember. I wouldn't have thought it of him, but you saw how wasted he looked. You never know what people will do if they get hungry enough."

"We've got to stop him," said Hyrum. "Whether he knows it or not, he's killing people."

"And if they don't die from typhoid, they die from starvation after the thieves clean them out," Mason added grimly. "Morty said it was Hank's idea for him to bring people food. Remember the crackers? Morty must be telling him who he visits, and then Hank sends his guys a few weeks later to clean them out."

Dee counted back, trying to remember how long it had been since Morty stopped by. "It's been a little over three weeks. If there's going to be a break-in here, it'll be soon."

"How many guns do we have?" said Mason. "I think I've got an idea."

*

Grandpa didn't like the plan, which involved luring the thieves into the house to corner and capture them. He said they'd be better off just shooting at them from the house and scaring them off.

"With all respect, if we do that then they'll just go after someone more helpless than we are or come after us later when we aren't expecting it," said Hyrum, who thought Mason's plan would work. "Right now we have the advantage since we know they're coming and we're not as sick as they think."

Reluctantly, Grandpa agreed that capturing the thieves was the right thing to do. Dee was worried, too, but she couldn't stop thinking about Courtney's three girls. "I don't think we have a choice," she said finally.

Angela, Joseph, and the younger children were ordered to stay upstairs with Jasper and keep out of sight while Grandpa, Hyrum, Mason, Dee, and Jeremiah got things ready. They were careful to stay away from the windows. If the house was being watched, it needed to appear as if they were all sick inside.

Grandpa and Mason checked the guns. They had three—Grandpa's shotgun, Mason's revolver, and the pistol he'd put in Dee's backpack on the day of the EMP. Dee didn't want anything to do with the gun, so they decided Hyrum should carry it.

The kitchen had three doors—one that led to the hallway and entryway, one to the dining/living room, and one to the porch. They all agreed that the invaders were most likely to come through the porch and into the kitchen to get to the food more quickly. To encourage the use of the porch entrance, they left the outer door slightly ajar as an invitation.

Dee climbed down into the cellar and draped sheets and towels over their food storage. There wasn't time to move it, but they didn't want to advertise they had it, either. After she finished, Mason pulled the ladder up entirely and hid it out of sight in Grandpa's room. Leaving the trap door all the way open so it rested on the floor, Hyrum laid the rug carefully over the hole to disguise it, making it into a pit trap.

Mason walked everyone through the plan. "I think we should tie Jasper near the front door. That way they're almost certain to come in through the patio door instead. I'll be under the table; the tablecloth will hide me. We'll leave the door to the pantry open and they should make a beeline straight over there. At least one of them will fall into the cellar, two if we're lucky, and then all of you are going to come through the other two doors."

"What if we come in at the wrong time?" asked Jeremiah.

"Once their guy falls in the cellar it will be chaos. You'll know when it's time. You and Hyrum will be in the living room. Doc Kerns and Dee will be in his room. Each pair has a gun. When you hear the racket, come into the kitchen and point your weapons at the thieves but don't get close. Dee, you light the lamp and they'll see we've got them. There's no way out, they'll be short a guy, and they'll have three guns on them."

"What are we going to do with them then?" asked Dee. She was starting to have some doubts now, as well. What if the thieves were better armed than they were?

"They'll be trying to get their guy out of the cellar so they won't have any weapons out. That makes it a lot easier. We'll take their guns and tie them up, and then we can try and find out who's in charge of this whole thing."

Dee knew Grandpa wasn't sold on the plan. He just wanted to take care of them and keep everyone under his roof safe. He hadn't seen what had been done to Courtney, or to Mason's mom. Dee had, and she knew they had to try to stop it.

*

Dee was napping on Grandpa's bed when the sound of the doorbell woke her. "Shh," Grandpa said. "It's almost time." She was wide awake in an instant as adrenaline rushed through her. The doorbell stopped and she figured Hyrum or Jeremiah had cut the wire, but Jasper still barked. Her hands were icy and she felt like she could barely breathe, but Grandpa put a steadying hand on her shoulder. Together they crept out of his room and into the hallway, where they listened through the kitchen door, waiting for their cue.

Dee heard a stifled scream, a thud, and then panicked voices—this was it! Grandpa went first, shotgun in hand. With shaking hands she struggled to light the lamp. The door was really close to the pantry and once she turned up the lamp, she had a perfect view of the scene in front of her.

A man was on his knees in front of the pantry, grasping the arms of another man whose legs and lower torso dangled into the hole in the floor. From below, she heard muffled moans of pain, and then the man who was halfway through the hole yelled, "Get me out of here!"

"Hold it right there," said Grandpa in a loud voice, his shotgun pointing directly at them. "Hands where I can see 'em."

The man on his knees slowly turned and when he saw the barrel of the shotgun aimed at him he put his hands up.

"I'm slipping, don't let go!" the man in the hole shouted, until he too caught sight of the gun.

The man in the kitchen twitched, as if thinking about going for a weapon, but he froze when he heard Mason's voice behind him say, "I wouldn't do that if I were you."

The men's heads swiveled around and they caught sight of Hyrum and Mason. "I'm going to make sure the patio and backyard are clear," Mason said.

Grandpa nodded in his direction without taking his eyes off the thieves. "Listen up. When I tell you, you're going to slowly take out your weapons, put them on the ground, and push them this way. If there's any monkey business I'll tell you right now that I would dearly love an excuse to fill you clean full of shot. Go on," he said. "Nice and slow."

Dee heard the sound of feet on the stairs behind her. It was Sammy and Katy, running down in their pajamas. "We've gotta get Jasper," Sammy whispered as they rounded the bottom of the stairs and headed for the front door. Dee realized the barking had gone quiet.

"No, Sammy, wait . . ." she said, but they were already at the front door.

Grandpa hadn't heard the kids go by, and now he said, "Maddie, get down and pull those guns closer. Stay out of my sights."

Dee hesitated, glancing behind her. The doorway was clear, and Mason would be around in a minute on his sweep. "Come on, Maddie," Grandpa urged. She dropped to her knees and gingerly picked up the two weapons, careful not to block Grandpa's shot. As she stood back up she heard a click behind her.

Dee looked quickly down the hallway to the front door. The swinging lantern light showed a man locking the door. When he turned to face her she saw he held a gun to Katy's head.

"Tell the old man to put down the gun or the little girl gets it," the man said without a trace of fear. Dee had no doubt he meant what he said. Grandpa was already lowering his gun.

"All of you, put the guns down and go stand by the table. Move it!"

Dee looked at Katy's terrified face and did what the man said. Soon, he had Hyrum's pistol, too. "No one's going to get hurt as long as you do what I say." Something about the man's voice sounded familiar and she tried to see him better in the dancing shadows. A flicker of light glanced off his enormous belt buckle and Dee fought to smother a gasp as she recognized the man who'd caught her trying to rescue Mason at the church—Mitchell. She glanced up at Hyrum to see if he'd made the connection and he gave her a slight nod, his face grim.

There was no sign of Mason, and Dee wondered what he was doing outside.

As if he could read her mind, Mitchell said with a sneer, "Your friend outside is down for the count." He patted a second gun tucked into his belt, and Dee saw with horror that it was Mason's.

While they watched, the two guys were pulled out of the cellar and began loading the food supplies from the pantry.

"Anything down there?" Mitchell asked the man who'd fallen all the way in. He was sitting off to the side, nursing a hurt foot and glaring at anyone who dared look at him.

"Why don't you go see for yourself," he snapped.

"Watch yourself, Martin," warned Mitchell, "or you'll be walking back to town. You might have to anyway, because I'm thinking about bringing along that lovely young lady over there." He indicated Dee with a nod of his head. "I know someone who wants to get to know her better, and I think he'll have a nice thank-you present for whoever brings her in. Between her, that punk outside, and the little kid, I think I'll earn my very own bottle of Wild Turkey before morning."

"Take the food," said Grandpa, "but you're not taking the children."

"Is that right, old man?" said Mitchell, bringing the gun around to point at Grandpa. "And who's going to stop me?"

At that moment, Angela stepped through the hallway door and into the kitchen behind Mitchell, smashing him over the head with Grandpa's crystal ball cane.

"I am," she said, as he crumpled to the floor.

CHAPTER TWENTY-ONE

It seemed to Dee that the whole world froze. Angela bent over and picked up Mitchell's gun. The rest of the weapons were still in the bag at his feet. "Get on the floor!" she yelled at the men in the kitchen. They stood staring, not sure what to do.

Angela leveled the gun at the nearest man and said in the same carefully controlled voice Dee had heard her use with her children when she was especially cross with them, "One."

The man prostrated himself on the floor, suddenly in a huge hurry to comply. "Two," said Angela, and clicked off the safety.

The other men were on the floor before Angela got to three. Hyrum grinned. "Nice timing, Mom."

Dee heard the roar of an engine and snatched up one of the guns and sprinted for the front porch. Sammy and Mason were still in trouble. She threw the front door open, but it was too late. A dirty tan pickup was racing down the lane, spitting up rocks and slushy mud as it made its escape. Mason chased after it but the truck pulled away easily, leaving him to stagger along behind.

Dee didn't dare take a shot, afraid she'd hit Mason. When she finally caught up to him he was standing with slumped shoulders and blood flowing freely from a gash in his forehead. He turned to face her and she took an inadvertent step back, startled by his eyes—black and full of fury.

She expected him to yell or scream, but his voice was tightly coiled. "Hank's behind all of this and now he's got Sammy. I'm going to kill him."

*

Back at the farm, Hyrum and Jeremiah finished tying up the men and Grandpa checked Mitchell for a pulse.

"I didn't kill him, did I?" Angela asked, a worry line creasing her forehead.

"No, and it's a real shame. This feller's not worth the clothes he's wearin'. Mason, Hyrum, help me take this scum out to the barn and tie them inside the cattle trailer. We'll lock it up tight. That ought to hold 'em." He looked at Mason. "After that we'll come up with a way to get Sammy back."

Mason paced anxiously. "There's no time. I just need a gun and then I'm out of here." He put a hand to his forehead and touched the dried blood there. "I'm such an idiot. Mitchell clocked me while I was trying to get the jump on his driver. Then they grabbed Sammy while I was down. I've got to go after him, he's just a kid." Dee saw Mason's lip tremble as he turned away. "He's the only family I've got left."

"Listen, son," said Grandpa, putting a gnarled hand on Mason's shoulder. "I'm not going to try to stop you. You and Sammy are like my own kin now. But I don't think you should go rushing in without some backup."

"I'm not risking anyone else. This is between me and Hank."

"Sammy's part of our family now, too. Don't ask me to stay behind." Hyrum crossed his arms across his chest and gave Mason a look that said, "I dare you to try and stop me."

Dee reached for Grandpa's hand and gave it a squeeze. His eyes were warm on hers and she knew he understood. She looked at Mason. "I'm ready when you are."

Angela looked up from where Katy was petting Jasper. He'd had the wind knocked out of him but didn't seem otherwise injured. Dee wondered if Angela would object to the rescue mission, but she just said quietly, "It's my fault they took Sammy. He and Katy slipped away when my back was turned. I'm so sorry, Mason."

"It wasn't your fault." Mason pulled Angela to his chest for a tight hug. "Don't you worry. We're going to get Sammy back."

*

It didn't take long before they were ready to go. Mason and Hyrum both had backpacks with supplies they thought they might need, and they all had guns. The pistol Mason had given Dee felt heavy in the holster he had stripped from one of Hank's men. She wondered if she'd have the guts to use it if she had to.

It was late afternoon and cool shadows reached across the road. As they came up to the roadblock they got out of the truck to scope it out, but it was unmanned. The fire truck had been moved and they had no trouble pulling the truck around it. They drove slowly into the silent town in the deepening twilight.

Mason had drawn a map of what he could remember of the police station's layout, and they had a basic plan. Dee smiled wryly at the absurdity of calling it a *plan*. The idea was to break in, grab Sammy, and get away, but they didn't know how they would get in, where Sammy was being held, or how they were getting out. He might not even be at the police station.

Dee noticed Mason clenching and unclenching his fists and put a hand on his arm. "We're going to get him back."

There were no lights in any of the windows or smoke coming from the chimneys of the houses they passed. She wondered if they were empty or if people were hiding inside.

As they drove quietly through the empty streets, Dee steeled herself for what was coming. A year ago she wouldn't have believed she'd be on her way to break into a police station with her boyfriend and her best friend. A year ago she'd been drowning in her own self-pity over the loss of her brother. Now here she was, ready to risk her life for a little boy who was like a brother to her.

Maybe what she was about to do wasn't so surprising, after all.

They parked the truck a couple blocks away from the station and then crept through the cars still scattered around the parking lot of the urgent care center. The two-story building next door looked like a fortress. The fire station took up most of the lower floor, and the police station comprised the second story.

Dee felt her stomach clench tightly. They had to be crazy to try to break into a police station. Their breath was visible as puffs of white in the chilly evening air and Dee wondered if Sammy was warm enough. She glanced at the other two to see if they were ready.

Hyrum whispered, "Do you mind if we say a prayer first?"

Dee expected Mason to make a snarky comment about it and was surprised when he nodded. "I wish I had your faith, man, but if your God listens to you, we need all the help we can get."

The prayer was short and to the point, and Dee and Mason both added their *Amen* when it was over. She didn't know if God would help them or not, but the tense bundle of nerves in her stomach had relaxed somewhat and she felt like they might have a chance. Hopefully Mason was feeling it, too.

"I guess this is it," Hyrum said. "You guys ready?"

From outside they could see a guard sitting at the desk in the lobby. They couldn't get in that way. Instead they circled around to the fire bay. The tall garage doors were all rolled down and secured, and when Mason tried the smaller side door into the fire station it was locked.

"Just keep going around," Mason whispered. "There's another door near the fitness center."

Door after door was locked and Dee wanted to scream in frustration. They reached the last door, but it was behind a chain-link fence that enclosed a small patio and gravel area. Hyrum looked at the fence and rubbed his chin. "Is there any point climbing over this thing? I'm sure they've got that door locked, too."

"Probably," said Mason. "We've got to find some other way in. Maybe we can lure the guard outside." They all knew the guard was sure to sound an alarm, and then they'd lose their only advantage.

Dee looked at the enclosure more closely. There wasn't a gate in the fence, but it wasn't topped with razor wire, either. "What was this little area for, anyway?" she asked and then wrinkled her nose. "It stinks."

"That door goes into the kennel for the K-9 unit. The dogs could come out here to pee." Mason's expression brightened and he peered through the fence. "I forgot about this," he whispered excitedly. "There used to be a doggy door so they could go in and out."

Dee could see it now. A medium-sized door flap was installed in the lower half of the door.

"It's worth a try," said Hyrum. "Hold on, I'll check it out first."

He scaled the fence and dropped down lightly on the other side. No luck with the door handle. Dee held her breath while he tried the doggy door. It swayed slightly at his touch and Dee suppressed an excited shout. Crouching down, Hyrum pushed it open and peeked inside, and then gave a thumbs-up. "It's dark in there, no guards."

Mason and Dee climbed over the fence while Hyrum tried to reach through the dog flap and unlock the door from the inside.

"It's no use, I can't reach."

"Here, let me try," said Mason, shouldering in. Dee scanned the area and saw a flickering light bobbing along near the fire bay.

"Someone's coming!" she whispered.

Mason strained, but he couldn't reach the handle, either.

Dee looked back at the flashlight. It was getting closer and would be on them any second. She looked at the small opening doubtfully. She took off her coat and sweater, feeling the night air cool the thin layer of sweat on her skin.

"No laughing," she warned the others, and then stuck her arms and head through the door. She got through as far as her hips, but the opening wasn't wide enough. Even though their situation was grave, she felt a sudden urge to giggle at what she must look like from outside. The dog door was taller than it was wide, and if she could just turn sideways, maybe she could squeeze through that way. Awkwardly, she twisted her body through the narrow door and then felt her hips clear the opening. She fell heavily onto her side and then turned and pulled her legs and feet in the rest of the way.

She was up instantly, feeling her way along the door. She found the doorknob and twisted the lock. The handle turned but the door wouldn't budge. There had to be another lock. Quickly she ran her hands over the door and found a deadbolt. It turned and the door opened. Mason and Hyrum crowded inside with her. Once they were in, they eased the door closed and Dee got down on the ground to peek through the doggy door at the guard. He strolled along casually and she didn't think he'd heard them.

They were in.

CHAPTER TWENTY-TWO

Mason and Hyrum were already creeping down the hallway and Dee hurried to catch up. One hallway branched off to the right, and a few feet farther down another branched left. Mason put a finger to his lips and looked down the first hallway. In a voice so low she could barely hear him he whispered, "Lobby. The guy at the front desk has his back to us." Then he indicated the hallway that led left. "The holding cells are down that way. You stay here while I check it out." He didn't give them any time to argue, and he was back moments later with a shake of his head. "They're using them for storage. Sammy's probably upstairs." He motioned toward the hallway on the right. "Stairs are this way."

Dee dared a glance around the corner and saw the steps leading upstairs. To get to them, they'd have to sneak behind the guard at the front desk without making a sound. "One at a time," whispered Hyrum. "I'll go last. And if we get split up, meet out front with Sammy."

Mason rounded the corner and Dee watched as he made his way quietly to the stairs. Once he got there she glanced at Hyrum. He gave her a reassuring smile and a nod. "I'll be right behind you."

Dee was halfway to the stairs when the guard cleared his throat. She froze and watched as he took a sip from a mug and set it back down next to his keys on the desk. A pool of lantern light filled the lobby, and if he turned his head he would see her. Then he'd catch her and give her to Hank. The thought of being at Hank's mercy kept her frozen in her tracks. She couldn't move.

She was going to ruin everything. She had to go. With another anxious look at the guard she took a step forward and then another and another until she reached the stairway. She turned back to see if Hyrum was following, but his head was low to the floor and he made desperate motions with his hands. Just then she heard the guard's chair squeak. He was getting to his feet.

Had he heard them? Mason grabbed her hand and they raced silently up the stairs, listening for the sound of footsteps in pursuit. They came out in another dark hallway and Mason pulled her into the nearest room, where they stood breathlessly waiting. Dee could feel Mason's heart thudding as loudly as her own, but they didn't hear anyone coming up the stairs.

Instead, they heard the guard unlock the front door and let in another guard. Probably the one who had been on patrol. Dee wondered if he patrolled inside, too. If so, they were in trouble. But she needn't have worried. The two guards chatted in the lobby, and for the moment it seemed they were safe.

Dee turned her flashlight on and shone it around the room. They were in some kind of kitchen or break room. A fridge loomed in the back corner next to several open, and empty, cupboards. A wall-mounted first aid kit had also been stripped bare.

"Let's go," said Mason.

They came out into a long hallway with the break room behind them, the stairs in front of them, and an open area to their right with a high ceiling and a railing that overlooked the lobby below.

They couldn't see the guards but they could hear them talking about the raid on the farm earlier.

"I'd stay out of Hank's way if I were you," said the lobby guard. "You should have seen him when Rasmussen walked in alone with just the boy."

"Wasn't he glad to get his kid at least?" said the patrolman.

"And lose half his team without a scrap of food or supplies to show for it? No kid's worth that."

The patrolman grunted in agreement.

Dee was counting in her head. Back at the farm they'd caught Mitchell, the two guys that had fallen in the cellar plus one more. Four. If that was half of Hank's men, and two of them were downstairs, it meant there were two more men upstairs and one of them was Hank.

She looked at the long dark hallway off to her left. That must be where they were, along with Sammy. Mason was already creeping that way, and motioned that she should follow. She hoped Hyrum was okay downstairs. She knew he wasn't going to be able to make it upstairs as long as the guards were both in the lobby.

Dee could see a dim light down one direction and pointed it out. Mason nodded and headed that way. They passed another closed door and then came to a room with a glass door they could see into. Several lanterns illuminated the room, and Dee could see a large whiteboard, a map of what she assumed was Lookout Falls, and several empty desks. One man lounged on a couch while he thumbed through a hunting magazine.

A door near the back spilled light into the room. Hank was probably inside, Dee reasoned. On the wall nearest them was a large interior window, and Dee saw that it looked into an interrogation room. A candle flickered inside and Dee could just make out a small form huddled under a blanket in the corner of the room. It was Sammy, she was sure of it.

Mason had her by the hand and pulled her back down the hallway a few steps to the unopened door. It probably led into the interrogation room. Dee held her breath while Mason tried the handle. She wasn't surprised when it was locked.

"We've got to get the key," whispered Mason.

Dee thought about the room next door. If they went in with their guns they might be able to force the guard on the couch to give them his keys, but if he raised an alarm they'd have the downstairs guards on them, as well as Hank. It would probably be a bloodbath and no guarantee they'd even get the keys. There had to be another way.

The sound of the guards chatting in the lobby drew her attention and she remembered seeing a ring of keys on the guard's desk. Were they still there? Quickly, she whispered to Mason what she was thinking and he followed her down the hallway. When they got close to the railing Mason lowered himself to his stomach and crawled up to the edge. He looked down at the desk and then gave Dee a thumbs-up before slithering back.

"His keys are on the desk, and they are sitting on easy chairs over there," Mason pointed to one side of the lobby. "I'm going to crawl in and get them. If I move real slow they might not see me."

"But what if they do?"

"If they do, I'll grab the keys and toss them up to you. You should have enough time to hide in the break room before the guards up here run past, and then you can use the keys to get Sammy out."

Even if Mason got the keys to her, if he was seen he'd be taking on four trained cops at once. He wouldn't stand a chance. And once she got the door open and Sammy out, where would she go?

It wasn't a very good plan, but she didn't see any other way to get the keys. It was too bad they couldn't levitate them straight up.

"Wait a minute," she whispered, putting out a hand to stop Mason, who was already tiptoeing to the stairs. "What if we could get the keys from here?"

Mason shook his head. "Like a magician? Be serious. One of these guys is going to find us at any moment." He held out his hands in irritation and his wrist caught Dee's eye. She remembered the paracord bracelet he'd given her.

"Wait," she whispered excitedly. "What about this?"

Mason looked at her bracelet. "You might be onto something. How could we hook the keys with it, though?"

Dee inspected herself. In her pockets she had a few lucky pennies and the piece of gum she was saving. Nothing useful. "Maybe there's something in the break room."

Inside, Mason quietly searched through drawers but came up empty-handed. "We have to go back to the first plan," he finally said with a helpless shrug. "At least if they see or hear me I can toss the keys up to you and you can get Sammy. I'll try to draw everyone into the lobby so you can get out the back."

Dee scanned the room desperately. There had to be a way to keep Mason from sacrificing himself. Her eyes fell on the fridge. It wasn't big or fancy, but there were a lot of things stuck to the freezer door. She stepped closer and saw that the cops had been playing with magnet words. She read:

HAPPINESS IS COMPLEX BUT WHO CAN RELAX IN THIS INTENSE LY BITTER COLD WITH OUT BEER

Other types of magnets held outdated flyers and notices. Then it hit her: magnets! Would a magnet stick to keys?

Mason was already ahead of her. He grabbed a few magnets shaped like pushpins and tried to lift his keys with them. It took four or five together before it was strong enough, but it worked. The keys lifted from the counter with barely a sound. Quickly he tied the bundle of magnets to the end of the unraveled paracord bracelet and they crept back to the edge of the second floor overlooking the lobby.

Dee crossed her fingers as Mason slowly lowered the magnets. She watched the guards on the couch but they were deep in debate over whether football season would start up if the power came back on and which cities would still have teams. Luckily, their conversation was growing heated, and the sound of the keys clicking onto the magnet wasn't audible.

Dee's eyes were glued to the keys slowly inching toward them. The light from the lantern didn't reach very high and she doubted they'd be visible in the gloom if the guards looked over. But if Mason jerked the cord or moved it too quickly she knew the keys would crash to the desk and alert them. She held her breath and was surprised to see Mason's lips moving in a soundless prayer.

When the keys were almost to them Dee reached out and gently lifted them the rest of the way over. She glanced at the guards, still oblivious in their argument.

"Come on," mouthed Mason, as he slithered away from the edge.

Back in front of the interrogation room, Dee inspected the keys while Mason kept watch through the glass door. There were only three keys on the ring, and one was a strange square shape, so she ruled it out immediately. The second key fit the lock and it turned with a quiet click. Dee glanced quickly at Mason but he shook his head. The men hadn't heard.

Mason waved at her to keep watch while he crept in to get Sammy. She pocketed the keys and saw that the guard from the couch stood in the back doorway talking to someone in the rear office. If he turned he'd be able to see Mason through the one-way glass. So far, so good. She watched as Sammy sat up and saw Mason. Mason put a finger to his lips and the brothers quietly crept out of the room. Dee couldn't believe their luck. They had Sammy, and now all they had to do was sneak out the back and find Hyrum.

She should have known it was too good to be true.

She saw a circle of light on the break room door getting larger just as her ears registered the sound of someone climbing the steps. Someone was coming upstairs and there was nowhere for them to hide.

They were about to be discovered.

CHAPTER TWENTY-THREE

Mason moved swiftly to the top of the stairs and waited. When the patrolman appeared, Mason hit him in the face with his flashlight and the stunned guard toppled backward down the stairs with a loud crash. "Come on," said Mason, racing after him.

Dee and Sammy followed quickly, and Dee heard the sound of raised voices and running feet down the hall. "The kid's gone," shouted a muffled voice. She and Sammy raced down the stairs past the fallen guard who groaned and struggled to get up. Mason grappled with the guard from the desk. He slugged him in the stomach, and the guard bent over in pain, but straightened up, throwing an uppercut that glanced off Mason's jaw.

She scanned the lobby and saw Hyrum outside the front door motioning for them to come out that way. Dee shouted for Mason and saw him land a blow to the guard's shoulder that knocked him into a wall. She ran for the front door and hit the push bar with a crash.

The door didn't budge. They were locked in.

Dee was terrified. She felt like her heart would pound its way out of her chest. She scanned the bar for a lock and saw a small square hole. The strange key on the guard's key ring would fit. In the reflection of the glass she saw Hank above them at the railing. He had a gun.

Dee fumbled for the keys in her pocket and with shaking hands. She fit the square key into the lock and turned. Mason yelled taunts, trying to keep Hank's attention off her and Sammy. He held the guard by the neck while he backed to the exit, the guard's body shielding Mason's. As Dee pushed open the door she heard gunshots and the guard Mason was holding screamed in pain. She and Sammy were out the door now and she hoped the glass behind them was bulletproof.

Grandpa's truck idled just down the street and Hyrum stood nearby, his gun out, ready to cover them.

"We can't outrun them in this," Dee said as she helped Sammy climb inside.

She saw Mason sprint out the front door and heard the report of Hyrum's gun as he fired on the station, trying to keep Hank and the other two cops inside.

"Hurry! I already took care of it," Hyrum said. At that moment a bullet grazed him along the thigh. He sagged and caught the truck door for support. Mason reached him and helped Hyrum in through the driver side door as another bullet shattered the glass in the rear window. Mason jumped behind the wheel and tires screeched as he gunned the engine.

Dee watched behind them as the cops ran onto the street. Hank ran after them while shooting, but he didn't land any more shots. The other two men raced around the building for their cars. As the truck passed the lot Dee saw flames leaping from a patrol car and the tan truck. In the flickering light reflected from the rearview mirror, Dee saw Hyrum smile.

Sammy looked worriedly at the blood soaking Hyrum's pants. He used his small hands to cover the hole until Dee could press her sweater to the wound. Hyrum gritted his teeth and Dee heard him force out the words, "'Tis but a flesh wound."

Mason shook his head with a grin and twisted the wheel. The truck shot around a corner and Hank and the police station became hidden from view.

*

As they neared the turnoff to the farm, Mason slowed and Dee saw that Angela was standing in the lane, motioning for them to stop. Behind her, Dee saw Jeremiah working a crowbar between the bars of the cattle guard.

Angela stepped closer to the truck to peer inside and Dee saw she was checking to make sure they were all there. Her relief was obvious. Hyrum manfully put on a brave face but in the dim light Dee could see he was pale and sweating.

"Are they following you?" asked Angela.

"They will be," said Mason, grim certainty in his voice. "Once Hank gets started on something, he never gives up."

"Then we'd better hurry with this. Milton suggested we lift out the cattle guard. Anyone driving this way won't suspect it's gone and will drive right into the hole. We've got it loosened, but we could really use the truck to power it out."

Dee opened her mouth to object. They needed to get Hyrum back to Grandpa so he could take a look at his leg, but Hyrum shushed her. "It can wait."

With the help of the truck they pulled out the bars of the cattle guard, leaving a square hole in the ground. Dee eyed the pit doubtfully. "Don't you think they'll notice?"

Angela was already spreading a large piece of burlap over the hole and securing the edges with rocks. Jeremiah scattered leaves and dirt over the top, and though it wasn't much Dee had to admit that in the dark it was effective. It only took a few minutes and then Angela and Jeremiah jumped into the back of the truck. "Let's go," she said through the back window.

When they got to the house Sammy slid out first and offered his small shoulder to Hyrum as support. Angela exclaimed over his leg and rushed to his side when she saw him hobble out of the truck. "I've had worse," he said with a glance at Sammy, giving the little boy's shoulder a squeeze. "Run see if there are any Spider-man Band-Aids left."

Sammy looked at him knowingly. "Your ouch is way too big for the Spider-man Band-Aids." He paused for a moment then searched Hyrum's face. "Do you mind one with Tinkerbell on it? They're bigger."

Sammy ran inside while Angela turned to Dee, Mason, and Jeremiah. "I'll get him inside. You guys keep a lookout and warn us when you see the truck lights go into the cattle guard. Milton says with the extra guns we took off Hank's men we've got enough firepower to hole up here and defend the house. We'll make our stand here, together."

After she went inside, Mason and Dee exchanged a glance. She knew Hank was dangerously angry, and she didn't want him anywhere near the house. What if he found his men in the barn? They'd be outnumbered then. No, they needed to head Hank off before he got close. Mason must have been thinking the same thing because he turned to Jeremiah. "Stay here and guard the house while I keep an eye on that cattle guard trap."

Mason didn't wait for Jeremiah's answer; he just started walking back down the lane. When Dee caught up with him he reached out to hold her hand as they hurried together into the darkness.

It wasn't long before they saw lights in the distance and heard the hum of an approaching car. They were hidden in the ditch next to the cattle guard, but it wouldn't provide much cover in a gunfight. Mason had his arm around her waist and she leaned into the warmth of his solid form. "I'm going to lure them up to the Searle place," Mason said. "There's cover and it's a good place to make a stand. You stay here and make sure no one makes it to the farm."

Did he really think she'd fall for that? Dee knew he was just making up a job to keep her out of the gunfight while he led the danger away.

Her pistol was still tucked down in its holster next to the pocket with the piece of gum she was saving and she wondered if she'd ever use either of them. She looked up at Mason, ready to object, and felt him touch her cheek. "Please let me keep you safe," he said softly.

In the light of the half-moon Dee saw his lips part as he leaned closer and kissed her gently. All thoughts of gum, guns, and Hank fled her mind as she savored the feeling of his work-roughened hand on her cheek and the soft pressure of his lips against hers.

It was over too quickly, and Dee didn't know if her heart was pounding more from the kiss or the danger rushing their way. As they watched, the car rounded the turn onto the lane and pitched almost full speed into the cattle guard trap with a loud crunch and the tinkle of breaking glass.

In the moonlight Dee saw two men stumble out of the vehicle. Mason stood up and ran past them toward the Searle house. His running steps crunched loudly in the gravel but they didn't go after him. They were busy trying to revive the driver, who was slumped over the steering wheel.

Dee watched Mason in the pale moonlight and saw him reach into his jacket pocket and pull his hand out empty. He checked another pocket, and then frantically checked all of his pockets. Her eyes widened as she realized he didn't have his gun.

"Leave him and let's go," one of the men ordered as they headed for Grandpa's house.

"Having some car trouble tonight?" taunted Mason.

What's he doing? she thought, even though she knew Mason would try anything to keep them away from Sammy.

"That little . . ." growled the man, and Dee's blood turned chill as she recognized Hank's voice in the darkness. "I'll take care of you later, boy!" The two men continued toward Grandpa's. They were past Dee now, too, and she didn't think they'd stop for anything.

Dee felt her heart beating in her throat and checked for her gun. She had to keep them away from the house and the prisoners. She got to her feet.

"You afraid of a girl, Hank?" she shouted. She heard Mason curse but her attention was focused on Hank. Would he follow her?

Dee could see him waver so she tried again. "If you catch me I'll tell you where your men are."

"When I catch you, you'll tell me anything I want to know," he growled and raced after her. Dee and Mason sprinted down the road toward the Searle house with the two men coming after them fast.

Dee realized that just ahead and to the right was the trail that led to the creek. "Follow me," she told Mason, and swerved off the road. "Hurry," she panted, and tried to find her way through the woods. The area looked a lot different from the way it had on the sunny autumn afternoon when she'd last been there, and she came close to panic when she realized the trail was covered with snow. She and Mason raced through the trees and Dee hoped they were heading in the right direction.

They stumbled into the picnic clearing and Dee took a moment to reorient herself before plunging straight back into the woods. She could hear Hank and his pal crashing through the underbrush after them and knew they weren't far behind. The snow was fresh and

Dee counted on Hank being able to track them easily. She didn't want him to give up.

Her flashlight shone ahead of her and she spotted what she was looking for—the bear cave. "We've got to make it look like we went inside," she told Mason between breaths. The two ducked under the low hanging rocks and quickly tracked partway into the cave. It was dark inside but not as cold. Dee looked deeper into the cave and she saw that it split in several directions. She wondered if Hyrum's dad had been right about the bear. She tossed her flashlight farther into the cave and signaled to Mason to go back out. The two stepped backward in their own tracks until they were outside the cave again. In the distance they saw flashlight beams dancing in the trees and she knew they didn't have much time.

"Come on," she said, hopping from one boulder to another until she found a place to climb up. Mason looked at her in disbelief but followed her, checking their trail to brush away any tracks. The dead tree leaning on the rocky ledge above the cave entrance provided scant cover, but it was enough. Hank barely looked up from their footprints.

The other man paused at the entrance to the cave. "Are you sure it's a good idea to go in there?" he asked, hesitation in his voice.

"If they were going to shoot at us they'd have done it already," snapped Hank. "That boy has had this coming for a long time. Maybe I'll let him watch while I convince his girlfriend to tell me where my men are. Who knows," he added in a sly voice, "maybe I'll even let you help me convince her."

The other man chortled and took a step into the cave. "You talked me into it, boss."

Dee waited several moments and then pushed against the dead tree. She was going to shove it away from the ledge so it fell and blocked the cave entrance. She pushed as hard as she could but the tree didn't budge.

"Are you crazy?" whispered Mason. "This is the plan? Come on. We need to get out of here before they come out."

"It'll work," Dee panted, heaving against the tree. She could swear she felt it give a little and tried to get more leverage. "It's right on the edge. All it needs is a little push."

Mason shook his head and leaned his shoulder into the log. "On three," he whispered. They pushed and this time she knew the log shifted. The sound was loud in the darkness and she heard the echo of pebbles falling to the ground below. Hank was sure to hear it, too.

Dee thought about Courtney and her little girls alone and starving, and she thought about Mason's mom dying in her own filth. It was time to put an end to Hank and his evil. "Come on," Dee prayed, and then together she and Mason pushed the log off the ledge. It landed with a thunderous crash right in front of the opening to the cave.

CHAPTER TWENTY-FOUR

On the way back to Grandpa's they saw that the driver of the car that drove into the cattle guard trap was gone. They picked up their pace, worried he might be a threat to the others, but when they reached the farm they found the man still passed out and now handcuffed in the cart. Grandpa cleaned the wound in his head while the others gathered around Mason and Dee to hear what happened in the woods.

"Are you sure they can't get out of the cave?" asked Hyrum, after they finished.

Dee noticed that he'd changed into soft sweatpants and leaned heavily on Grandpa's magic staff cane. "Yeah, the log wedged itself in tight, and there's no way they could squeeze past. We'll let them simmer down for a day or two and then get them out."

"What about the bear?" breathed Joseph, his eyes wide. "Did you see it?"

"That's just a story," Mason said, ruffling the boy's hair but not meeting his eyes. "There aren't any bears in these woods."

"That's not what my dad said," Joseph said, puffing out his chest with authority.

Dee didn't want to think about the low growls she'd heard coming from the cave, or the gunshots and then the screams they'd heard echoing all the way to the road. They'd go back and check the cave in a few days, but she knew there wouldn't be anything left of Hank or his friend.

"How about you?" she asked Hyrum, changing the subject. "How's the leg?"

"Nothing a little Tinkerbell Band-Aid couldn't handle," he said with a sidelong look at Sammy. The boy beamed. "It wasn't as bad as it looked," Hyrum added. "The bullet didn't go in, it just nicked me pretty badly. Your grandpa patched it up."

"Mason," said Grandpa, "can you give me a hand settling this fellow in the barn? His head's pretty banged up and I want to bed him down where I can check on him tonight."

"Sure thing," said Mason and towed the wagon toward the barn with Grandpa following after.

The others chatted in the yard for a while about the events of the night and then heard a sound coming from the house. Jasper was inside the screened patio barking for all he was worth. Sammy jumped up and down excitedly and clapped his hands. "Look at Jasper, he's all better!"

Dee raised her eyebrows at Hyrum.

"He wasn't doing so great when we got back from the station." He lowered his voice. "Your grandpa told Sammy he wasn't sure he was going to make it. Hank's man must have kicked him and started the bleeding again." Dee looked at the frantic dog on the porch and Hyrum added, "He doesn't usually bark like that, though, does he?"

Dee shook her head. "Not that I've seen. Maybe he's just glad we're all back." Even as she said it she knew it wasn't right. Jasper never barked like that. She looked around the yard and back down the lane. She gasped when something staggered out of the shadows toward them.

It was Hank.

His clothing was in shreds and he was covered in blood. His scalp was partially detached and dangled from one side of his head. Dee realized in horror that blood oozed from an empty eye socket.

The sight of the ruined man filled Dee with terror—and something else. Even though she was trembling with fear, she also felt bad for him, and a little guilty. She tried to make herself think of Courtney's little girls. They'd be alive if it wasn't for this monster. The man could barely walk, though, and he'd probably bleed to death if he didn't get help soon.

Hank looked them over until his gaze rested on Sammy. His voice came out in a hoarse whisper. "You ready to go home, son?"

Angela put her arms tightly around the two younger children. "It looks like you're hurt, Sheriff. Come over to the clinic and let Doc Kerns stitch you up."

Hank ignored her, his one eye seeking out and finding Dee. "Nice stunt at the cave, but I bet you didn't know there's a back way out. Of course"—he paused for effect—"it's hard to get to if you have to go around a really angry bear."

"I didn't know about the bear," Dee said. "I just wanted you to leave us all alone."

"Happy to oblige. Just give me my son and my men and we'll be on our way."

Dee looked over at Sammy; his face was hidden against Angela's leg. He'd already been through so much.

"Sammy stays with us." Hyrum's voice was firm.

"Sounds like you want me to shoot you again." Hank pulled a gun from his jacket pocket.

"Hank, listen," Dee said desperately. "We know about Morty and the typhoid. We know you used him to spread disease so you could steal food and supplies."

She saw she had his attention so she went on. "It's over now. It's all over. If this town is going to have a chance to survive, we need to stand together and stop hurting each other. You could help us."

"Do you have any idea how naïve you are?" Hank sounded irritated and combative. "The town won't survive. It's every man for himself. Survival of the fittest. You wouldn't last a day off this farm, out in the real world. Not"—he raised the gun to point it at her—"that you'll be around to find out."

Dee fumbled at her holster for the pistol and brought it up to point at Hank. He coughed out a laugh.

"Oh, so now you want to shoot me?" He took a step toward her and the gun wavered in Dee's grasp. "I don't think you have the guts."

For a fleeting moment she wondered if he was right. Then she gathered her resolve, closed her eyes, and pulled the trigger.

Or, at least she tried to. It didn't move.

She hadn't removed the safety.

Dee's hands shook as she looked at the weapon and tried to remember how to use it. Her mind was blank. Desperately she wished she'd accepted Grandpa's offer to teach her how to shoot.

"That's what I thought," came Hank's voice as he raised his weapon to point it at her. "You're not going to shoot me."

The barn door creaked loudly as it swung open. Grandpa stood outlined in the doorway, shotgun at his shoulder. "She won't, but I will."

The blast from the gun caught Hank squarely in the chest and he dropped heavily to the ground. With the echo of the gunshot still ringing in her ears, Dee turned to see Mason scoop Sammy up in one arm before embracing her tightly with the other.

It was over.

CHAPTER TWENTY-FIVE

The next day Mason hitched up the trailer with the prisoners and he and Dee drove them back to town. Grandpa didn't want them on the farm so he made the call to lock them up at the police station with some supplies until their futures could be decided. When Mason and Dee walked into the jail they were shocked to see a warehouse's worth of food stores and medical supplies stockpiled in the cells.

The prisoners were relegated to the K-9 kennels while they decided what to do with the food. Grandpa suggested they track down Max, the old fire chief. He called him a good man and said they could trust him to do the right thing. It seemed Grandpa's judgment of character was sound, because Max stepped into the role and brought on more honest men to sort the food and package it for immediate distribution.

Grandpa also insisted they drive him out to see Mr. Mortimer, the mail carrier. He said he intended to decide for himself whether Morty had been in on Hank's plan to infect the townspeople. After an hour-long conversation behind closed doors Grandpa declared Morty was all right and started him on a round of antibiotics to clear his system of the typhoid.

A couple days later Dee brought in some food Angela had prepared for the prisoners. It was the first meal they'd had after several days of surviving on MREs and they all dug in hungrily. Partway through the meal Morty walked in and said, "I'm glad to see you guys like my cooking." The look on Mitchell's face was priceless.

*

A week before Christmas, Dee sat in the office of the police station and marveled at how much had changed. The office was bustling with activity and Dee watched while Grandpa and the fire chief made plans for spring planting. Mason had been traveling around the countryside helping farmers repair old equipment to get it in working condition for spring, and the Searles had already traded some of their chickens for a baby piglet that would be born the following month.

Due to the weather and poor traveling conditions, the town didn't get a lot of visitors, but occasionally someone passing through brought letters or rumors of the world beyond their borders. According to the stories, lawlessness and disease ran rampant. A splinter group had formed in central Washington led by a political extremist. It was working its way east, looting farms and conscripting youngsters as it went. There were fragments of information about a large military force assembling in Reno and preparing to invade north, and a small group of rogue terrorists was on a murder spree just north of Seattle. Rumor had it they were the ones who launched the nuke that caused the EMP.

Max talked about them forming their own militia to defend the town and Dee decided she would join. She had grown to love Lookout Falls and wanted to learn how to use a gun and protect the town. She also prayed daily with Hyrum and his family that one day soon they'd get news from her parents and their oldest son in California. She knew their chances were slim, but she wouldn't give up hope.

The map of the town on the wall above Dee was studded with colored pins showing which houses had survivors. Grandpa always became very quiet when he looked at the many pinless parts of the map. When the census reports first started coming in he'd often been the one placing the pins as names of the dead and the living were read off.

The elderly were hit especially hard by the disaster. No one with a pacemaker had survived as long as he had. Diabetics, everyone on dialysis, many cancer patients, and basically anyone heavily dependent on drugs to keep them alive were gone now. Grandpa told her he was glad Grandma Madeleine wasn't alive to see the sad fates of so many of their close friends.

The poor side of town was also devastated. Sickness and disease swept easily through the closely situated homes and apartments, and with winter in full force most were finding it difficult to stay warm in the poorly insulated buildings. The fire chief estimated that at least sixty percent of the population was gone, and they'd lose more over the winter.

Dee knew a lot of people had died, but it gave her hope to see so many pins on the map. Many people were still fighting to stay alive. She placed a finger on the pinless square representing Courtney's house and swore to herself she'd do all she could to help people survive.

That afternoon Dee and Mason were scheduled to make some food deliveries, but when it was time to go there was no sign of him. "I'm sure he's just late getting back from the Morris farm," Grandpa reassured her. "Why don't you head out that way and make sure he hasn't had any car trouble. And no deliveries by yourself." So far people had been grateful to receive the food, but Grandpa and

Max were always careful to make sure the delivery drivers could be trusted and none of them traveled alone.

Max added, "Come on back if you don't see him and we'll send out a party."

*

Dee had barely reached the outskirts of town when she saw a lone figure walking on the side of the road.

She pulled the truck up next to Mason. "Do you know the way to the nearest train station?"

"I see you still haven't learned your lesson about picking up strange guys on deserted highways," he said, grinning, and climbed in.

Dee shook her head. "You'd think I'd learn. The last time I did I wrecked the truck."

Mason reached into his pocket and pulled out a small box. "I made you something." He held it out to her.

She took it, protesting. "But Christmas isn't until next week. I don't have your present yet."

"I can wait, and besides, if you don't open it now Sammy is going to blurt out what it is and spoil the surprise. Go on, open it."

She lifted the lid and smiled. Nestled on a piece of tissue paper was a bracelet made of blue and white paracord.

He took it out and showed it to her. "The clasp has a built-in whistle. It's smaller than my old one, too. I hope it fits okay."

Dee raised her wrist and he snapped it on. It was perfect. A glint of silver caught her eye, and she turned the bracelet around for a better look. Near the clasp was a tiny charm that said *Believe*.

"Do you like it?" he asked, watching her hopefully.

She looked at him, with his long lashes and wavy hair that begged for a haircut. The expression in his dark eyes was warm.

"I love it," she said.

"My thoughts exactly." He slid across the seat toward her. His leg brushed hers and she felt a tingle rush through her body. She looked up and saw that he was leaning down to kiss her. She thought briefly of the gum in her pocket and then raised her lips to his.

Next time, she promised herself, knowing there would be many more.

AFTERWORD: PREPAREDNESS AND EMPS

I've had a surprising number of people come to me after reading *Outage*, asking what they need to do to prepare for the worst. Many of them are just realizing they aren't ready for a disaster and they're anxious about it. If you're feeling this way I encourage you—don't get scared, get ready.

There's far more to preparedness than I could tell you in a conversation or a single book. Also, what one person wants or needs in a disaster isn't going to be the same for another, but I can tell you a few things you can do to get started.

The most important thing you can do is store or have a way to purify clean water for yourself and your family. Five gallons per person is the minimum place to start. Once you have that, make preparations for storing or purifying more.

Next, talk to your loved ones about an emergency plan. It doesn't have to be complicated; just make sure you're on the same page about where you'll meet or go or stay in an emergency.

Finally, you can buy or assemble what's known as a 72-hour kit for every person in your family. It's an easy-to-grab pack that contains three days of food, simple first aid supplies, and a few other survival items that may come in handy in a disaster.

Just having a few days' worth of food and water easily available to your family can make all the difference in the event of a major emergency in your area, including hurricanes, ice storms, earthquakes, tornados, etc. Although it's good to be aware of what an EMP is, you are far more likely to experience a natural disaster, so plan with that in mind.

A lot of what we think we know about EMPs is based on speculative science-fiction novels. Even *Outage* is just my own interpretation of what could happen. Until a first-world country experiences a massive and unexpected EMP, we probably won't know exactly how far-reaching and disastrous its effects could be.

I, for one, will be happy if we never find out. In the meantime, I'm doing a few basic things to prepare for the worst.

I hope you are, too.

~Ellisa

ACKNOWLEDGMENTS

I wrote most of *Outage* during National Novel Writing Month (NaNoWriMo) in November 2013. Thanks to Lisa Krebs for introducing me to the program and being my writing partner and unfailing friend, then and always. I encourage anyone who has ever wanted to write a novel to join this challenge next November.

No one was harder on my manuscript than I was, and I thank all my early beta readers for helping me fine-tune it, and finally convincing me they liked it. I self-published *Outage* in May 2014 and was blown away by the positive reception and great reviews it received. Thanks to all of you for your encouragement and making me feel like a real writer.

When I was contacted by Vivian Lee with Skyscape a few months later it was a dream come true. Working with everyone at Skyscape has been great, and I'd especially like to thank my editor, Clarence Haynes, for his insight, and Vivian, for her faith and vision.

Thank you to my mom and my sister, Lynzee, for their nonstop support and confidence. They make me feel like I can do anything. My kids and husband also deserve special thanks for putting up with me while I write. (Though my kids are pretty happy for the chance to play video games and eat junk food while I'm distracted!)

Finally, thank you to my Grandpa Rudd, the original rancher-farmer-veterinarian. He's a true cowboy and an inspiration to me in all things.

AUTHOR'S NOTE

If you enjoyed *Outage*, stay tuned for the next book in the Powerless Nation series, *Voyage*.

In this harrowing companion novel to Ellisa Barr's *Outage*, the devastating effects of an EMP attack are experienced all over again, only this time the story unfolds on a cruise ship far out to sea, where Dee's parents are on a trip to Alaska.

Fifteen-year-old Sena Morgan has just begun the voyage of a lifetime, but she'll never reach her destination. A terrorist-triggered EMP destroys the ship's power and communication systems and starts a fire onboard, leaving thousands of passengers stranded in the cold northern Pacific.

As food and water dwindle, strangers with a deadly secret are brought aboard the ship. Sena's only hope of survival is to get as far from them as possible, but at sea there's nowhere to run.

Sena meets a couple trying to get home to their daughter, Dee. Together they will face unspeakable challenges as they try to reunite with their families despite a terrifying new reality.

For more information, visit amazon.com/dp/B00MU0NVA4.

ABOUT THE AUTHOR

Ellisa Barr grew up in a small town in Idaho, even smaller than the fictitious town of Lookout Falls. In the summer, almost entirely cut off from friends and other entertainment, she became a voracious reader. When she misbehaved as a tween, her parents despaired of finding a suitable punishment, because the only thing she wanted to do was read. Finally they resorted to grounding her from books. Her friends thought she had the best parents ever. Ellisa agrees.

She lives with her husband, two children, a dog, and a cat in Southern California, where she homeschools her kids and knows just enough about prepping to prolong her agony in the event of the apocalypse.

Connect with Ellisa at www.facebook.com/ellisabarrbooks, and find preparedness tips and further information about new releases at www.ellisabarr.com.